F[...]
THE ALPHA

A BBW Paranormal Shifter Romance

JASMINE WHITE

About This Book

Evelyn has a dark secret. A secret so dark, that if her pack found out she could be sentenced to death.

However, now it could be time for the secret to come out.

Evelyn has been slated to marry Leon, the Alpha of her pack. Only she feels she can't. That is because she is love with someone else.

That someone else, is Jeremy, a wolf from a most-hated rival pack. The feud between the packs is almost at breaking point and this could be the incident that pushes everything over the edge.

Jeremy can not stand by and watch the woman he loves be married off to the Alpha. He knows he has to rescue his woman, even if he has to risk his life and face certain death to do so....

Read on for a gripping story of star crossed lovers, feuding shifters and furry heroes!

Get Yourself a FREE Bestselling Paranormal Romance Book!

Join the "**Simply Shifters**" Mailing list today and gain access to an exclusive **FREE** classic Paranormal Shifter Romance book by one of our bestselling authors along with many others more to come. You will also be kept up to date on the best book deals in the future on the hottest new Paranormal Romances. We are the HOME of Paranormal Romance after all!

* Get FREE Shifter Romance Books For Your Kindle & Other Cool giveaways

* Discover Exclusive Deals & Discounts Before Anyone Else!

* Be The FIRST To Know about Hot New Releases From Your Favorite Authors

Click The Link Below To Access Get All This Now!

SimplyShifters.com

CHAPTER ONE

The crackling fires clawed up toward the night sky almost as fiercely as the two furred beasts bit and clawed at each other. Everyone around me was shouting and cheering, filling the night with the sounds of bloodlust. We formed a circle around the two viciously fighting wolves, enjoying the show.

At least, most of us were enjoying it. I wasn't in the mood to be entertained by violence.

I was among the few who still had my clothes on. Most of the pack around me was naked by now, several of them with fresh wounds from having been in the ring already; others had taken their clothes off in anticipation of getting their turn. Some of them were just naked for the hell of it. It wasn't uncommon.

There were a few who were watching the fight in their four-legged forms. Every here and there among the humans standing around, was a wolf throwing his or her head back and howling, or just letting their tongues hang out. Now and then another one would join them, dropping to all fours and growing out their fur, their tails, and their protruding muzzles.

Everyone loved the fights. Most of the time I did too.

But not tonight.

Eventually, one of the competitors gained the upper ground, stepping over her opponent and baring her teeth, while the defeated party curled up beneath her with her tail between her legs. Victorious, the dominant wolf rose up on her hind legs, which extended into long human legs as her fur receded back into her flesh, and her snout shrunk back to form a human face, and long human hair extended from her head. Where there once was a drooling, sharp-toothed wolf, a nude, muscled human woman now stood before us, covered in fresh bites and scratches, and raised her fist in the air, giving a long, feral shout of victory. The rest of the pack howled and cheered with her; all except for her opponent, resuming her own two-legged shape while curled up in the dirt and crawling away.

And except for me.

I decided I'd seen enough, and turned and walked away. Watching the fight should have cheered me up, but it just wasn't working tonight. I guess that spoke volumes about my state of mind.

I didn't get very far before someone came running up behind me. I knew by her scent before I turned around that it was Charlene. Unlike me, she had long since ditched her clothes showing off all the scars she'd gotten participating in fights herself over the years. I had never been a fighter myself; I just liked to watch. Not to mention I liked my skin smooth and unscarred.

"Evie, where you going?" she asked. "Aren't you having fun?"

"Can't really get into it tonight," I shrugged. "Guess I got too much on my mind."

"Yeah, that figures," Charlene sighed. "If I were in your place… getting cold feet?"

"I don't think I ever had warm feet about this to begin with," I said. "I've been going out of my mind about it all day."

"Didn't it make you happy when he announced it?" she asked. "Half the girls in the pack would've given anything to be in your shoes."

"I was a little too overwhelmed to be happy," I said. "I never expected this…"

"You're not thinking of refusing, are you?" she asked.

I sighed. "How could I do that? Leon is the alpha, and besides, my dad would disown me. The chance for his grandchild to be the next alpha? He'd never forgive me if I walked away from that."

Charlene looked at me sympathetically. "Maybe you just need some time to get used to it. You're just reeling from the shock of it all. Once that passes, you'll realize what a great deal you've gotten."

I shifted uncomfortably. "Maybe."

"You want to go for a run?" she offered. "Might clear your head."

I smiled. "You know, I think that's exactly what I need."

"Come on, girl, get those clothes off already! Let's go!"

She hurried off ahead of me, dropping down onto all fours as her body changed shape. Shaggy fur grew out from her skin as her hair receded, her ears moved up her head and reshaped into points, her hands and feet transformed into canine paws, and her mouth and nose extended into a long muzzle. She loped along a short distance before she stopped and looked back to me.

I finally started stripping my clothes off, too. I started after Charlene, walking at first, getting steadily faster the more articles of clothing I discarded. By the time my underwear finally hit the ground I was actually running, alongside Charlene's lupine form. And after only a few more running steps, I leaped forward, and began to shift into my four-legged form in mid-air. I had my hands extended out before me when I leaped but they were my paws when they reached the ground and propelled me forward.

I went from running with the wind rushing over my bare skin to running with the wind rushing through my fur. My claws dug into the dirt, pulling me forward much faster than my human legs ever could.

Together we dashed past trees and bushes, leaping over banks and roots. Birds and small animals scattered from our approach. Nothing could stop us, and nothing could catch us. Not even my worries.

Charlene was right. This was what I really needed right at that moment. I needed to be free.

Maybe because that was exactly what I felt like I wasn't anymore.

My thoughts couldn't stop coming back to the events of that day.

It had been a day like any other until that moment when my dad came into the house with that big proud smile on his face. When I asked him what was up, his response was to tell me that Leon wanted to see me in the circle, and that he had something very important to say. He was deliberately vague about it, but the giant grin he couldn't wipe off his face kind of worried me.

Appropriately so, as it would turn out.

When I got out to the circle, I was massively unnerved to find that the whole pack had gathered there. I'd been expecting Leon to have something he wanted to say to me privately, given how dad had been so secretive about it. This was something he wanted everyone there to hear. This could not have been good.

Leon was standing proud at his place of honor atop the large rock at the head of the circle, decked out in his brown leather jacket and his slicked-back hair. As I drew near, moving progressively slower as I got closer to the circle and grew steadily more nervous, Leon held out a hand, beckoning me to join him. My heart pounded with apprehension. I cautiously approached, taking his hand and stepping up with him onto the rock.

Then he turned to the pack. "My pack brothers and sisters," he said. "Serving you all as alpha has been one of the most rewarding experiences I could have asked for. But there comes a point in every wolf's life when he realizes he can't face all the trials of life alone. That's why I've come to a decision."

Then he turned to me, looking me straight in the eye. "Evelyn," he said. "I've chosen you. I want you to be my wife."

The whole pack erupted in cheers and howls. Many of the she-wolves had tears in their eyes, torn between being overjoyed for me and wishing they could be me. Me? I just couldn't breathe.

I felt like I'd been in a state of constant disbelief ever since. I kept waiting for someone to come along, wake me up, and bring me back to reality. Any minute now, this dream would disappear, and I would go back to being my own self-sufficient she-wolf with no expectations on my shoulders.

I was, wasn't I? That was my reality. It always had been. I was never one of those girls who spent ages dreaming about her wedding day. I never even imagined myself being married, and for that matter, I'd barely given any thought to ever having pups. Yes, I had plenty of sexual encounters with other members of my pack before, but I never looked at any of them in any long-term kind of sense. Let alone the alpha himself.

I'm not quite sure what Leon even saw in me. I certainly wasn't the hottest catch in the pack; sure, I had no scars, but I wasn't the only one who could claim that. And there were others in that category who were a lot hotter than me. I was too curvy, for one thing; I'd been telling myself for years to lay off those snacks. And I had too many freckles, too. And hell, Charlene pulled off the curly brunette look better than I did; I always seemed to have some frizz hiding somewhere, and my split ends just didn't want to go away. So what was it about me that made him single me out?

Of course, my brain kept wanting to answer, "Dad suggested it."

The hours kept ticking by, and I had yet to wake up. That moment with Leon on the rock in front of the pack had still happened. I was still promised to become Mrs. Alpha of the Pack.

Still… as shocked and overwhelmed as I was about the whole thing, I wasn't completely sure I didn't want it either. Many times throughout the day I contemplated the idea of what being married to Leon would be like.

Honestly, when I really considered it, the possibility didn't seem that bad. Being the wife of the alpha was a good role to have. Everyone would look up to me; I would be in a position of power, with influence over the whole pack. My pups would have that same kind of influence after me.

I liked Leon. I really did. I'd always looked up to him and given him the respect he was due as an alpha. I even enjoyed his company from time to time.

I just did not love him.

Charlene and I ran until we tired ourselves out. I gradually slowed to a trot, and then stopped and sat, while Charlene lay down on the ground, sphinx-like. I spent a while catching my breath, my tongue hanging out, before Charlene finally turned her head to look up at me. She shifted her position to allow her legs to reshape in the right direction as she returned to her two-legged shape, lying on her side on the ground. "You feel better?" she asked me.

I shifted back to my own two-legged form, and then sat back, putting my hands behind me to lean on. "Yeah, a little," I said. "I needed to loosen up."

But of course, a little run didn't change my situation.

"What do you think you're gonna do?" she asked me. "You gonna go through with it?"

I shrugged. "I can't imagine I'd have the guts to say no," I said. "Now that everyone's expecting it, I can't let them all down."

"But is it what *you* want?"

I hesitated, taking a minute to think before I answered. "Maybe it will be. Once I get over the shock, like you said. Maybe once I think about it, I'll decide it's exactly what I want. I ought to at least give it a chance."

"That's the spirit, girl!" she grinned, reaching over to pat me on the leg.

It was pretty clear what side of the fence Charlene was on about this issue. I was more than sure most of the pack shared her sentiments.

I just wished I could make myself share them.

*

After I woke up from a fitful night's sleep the next day, I came out to the kitchen to find Mom making a batch of pancakes. She looked up at me and smiled as I entered. "Good morning, Mrs. Alpha," she beamed.

I made a face as I churned the strange taste of that through my mouth. "That still sounds weird," I said.

"Good weird?" she pried. Then cautiously she tried, "Bad weird?"

I shrugged. "I don't know. Just weird."

She flipped the pancakes she was cooking. "I'm making your favorite this morning," she said, still wearing that big smile. "Buttermilk pancakes, and I got you some powdered sugar and strawberries!"

Well, I knew I could be happy about that, at least. "Thanks, Mom," I relented, taking a seat at the kitchen counter. I watched her work, bringing her culinary craft to life. Mom was always a master in the kitchen; I could never quite measure up. Most of the stuff I tried to cook usually ended up as kindling for the bonfires. Well, they might as well have, if I didn't see fit to chuck them in the garbage first.

I just hoped Leon wasn't planning to have me cook for him.

Oh, crap... I'd just imagined myself actually being married to him. I didn't know if that was a good thing or not.

I decided not to dwell on it as I saw Mom stack up my breakfast on my plate, topping it with sugar and strawberries and sliding it toward me. When I dug into that stack, my worries, doubts, and uncertainty were allowed to melt away in the face of sweet, fruity heaven. They were almost as good as my little run had been last night.

I was able to lose myself in the food until I heard the door open and approaching footsteps, accompanied by my dad's scent. I lifted my head to see him coming into the room, looking at me with that same proud grin on his bearded face he had yesterday. Except now I knew what it was about. He didn't say anything; he just stepped up behind me and placed a hand on my shoulder.

"Did he just decide this yesterday?" I asked him. "Or were you planning this with him for weeks?"

Dad shrugged. "Well, I may have suggested you'd be a good match for him. You should be happy, darling. I put in a good word for you with the alpha, and it paid off. He picked you!"

I was tempted to say, "Did you wonder if I would've picked him back?" I refrained from saying that out loud. Dad would have looked at me as if I was from Mars if I said that. Rene Godfrey's only daughter not wanting to be married to the alpha? Just the suggestion would be enough to give him a coronary.

Honestly, the smiles all around were kind of unsettling to me. Especially Dad's. I knew from experience how quickly his happy look could turn to something far less pleasant. I didn't dare want to tempt that.

A chance for his bloodline to reach the coveted alpha position had been offered. To deny him that now would be the worst affront to him imaginable.

It was no secret that Dad had once challenged for the right of alpha back in his youth. It was years ago, before I was even born, so I'd only heard about it in stories. The stories all came from other members of the pack who were there at the time; Dad didn't like to talk about it himself. It was apparently his greatest shame.

From what I understood, the previous alpha died without an heir, and Leon's father and mine had each vied for the position. Or more specifically, they had *fought* for the position. As in with tooth and claw. Long story short, Dad lost. He'd apparently resented that loss ever since, and while he'd eventually made peace with the situation, and accepted Leon as alpha, once he became of age, and took over for his father, Dad had always hoped he could have a descendant take the position of power that he was denied.

So I didn't say anything more to him. I stuffed my face with a mouthful of pancake and chewed slowly.

Dad clapped me on the shoulder. "Come on, you look like you've got the world on your shoulders!" he thundered. "This is the best thing that's ever happened to you! Where's your smile?"

"Rene," Mom came to my defense, "leave her alone. This is a big deal. She needs time to process it."

Dad apparently still didn't get it. "What's to process? She should be jumping up and down instead of sitting here all mopey!"

"Rene!" Mom demanded, exercising the one source of authority besides Leon that Dad respected. "Give her some breathing room."

Dad grimaced, and walked away. "Well, I guess I'll go chop some wood while you process," he said, and disappeared out the front door.

I turned back around with a sigh. "Thanks, Mom."

Mom placed a hand atop mine. "This is very sudden for you, isn't it?" she said. "You're being asked to take on a big role that you didn't prepare for. But you still have a lot of time. You can get used to the idea."

I turned a vulnerable look up at her. "I don't know if I want to get used to it," I said weakly.

Mom gave me a look of understanding. "You don't love him," she acknowledged. "I get that. You know, love isn't always like it is in romance novels or

John Hughes movies. It doesn't happen all at once in some miraculous moment like a fireworks display. It takes time. You build it up, day by day. Like laying bricks. It took me a while to learn to love your father, you know."

Why doesn't that surprise me?

"I know this seems scary to you now," she went on. "But you can learn to love Leon if you try. It just takes time."

I appreciated what Mom was trying to do. I wasn't as comforted as she wanted me to be.

"Why don't you go talk to him today?" she offered. "Start laying some of those bricks."

I sighed. "Okay. I'll give him a chance."

*

After downing my whole plate, which had enough pancakes to feed three, I resolved myself to get some actual face time with the man who had been chosen to be my fiancée. Leon wasn't at home when I showed up at his door, but I followed his scent trail to old Tobias's garage. He was seated on the workbench with one foot resting on the seat below him, the other hanging free, as he watched Tobias, James and Terry working under the hood of Terry's rusty old pickup.

James lifted his head as I approached, and whistled to the others. "Heads up, fellas," he said. "Future Mrs. Leon is here."

Old Tobias slid out from underneath the truck. "Hey, hey, beautiful!" he chimed. "What brings you down to the grease pit?"

In response, I turned my attention toward Leon. "I was hoping I could borrow him for a minute?"

Leon smiled. "These old ratchet-heads were boring me anyway," he said, hopping down from where he sat. "I'm all yours."

As we walked out, Tobias made the quip, "Not even hitched yet and she's already got you whipped! Poor boy!"

"We'll see," Leon replied, turning his head back. "She doesn't seem so tough."

"Famous last words, buddy!" Terry said. "Famous last words!"

Leon and I put some distance between them and ourselves before he finally asked, "So, what did you want to talk to me about?"

I stopped. By golly, I had no idea what to say to him. "Well, I, uh… I… I just thought…"

"Yes?"

I shrugged. "Well, if we're going to be married, I thought we should have a chance to talk to each other."

"That's a wonderful idea," he said. Then he repeated, "So what did you want to talk to me about?"

And again, I was speechless.

"You're awfully tightlipped," he said. "You said you wanted to talk; don't you have anything to say?"

He wasn't being especially helpful. Searching for something, I craned my neck to look again to the garage in the distance. "What's wrong with Susie this time?" I asked, referring to the name given to Terry's rust bucket truck.

Leon looked back at it with me. "Tobias just replaced the transmission, and then there go the shocks again," he replied.

"Think the old girl's ready to be retired yet?"

"The old girl, I think she was ready to be retired years ago," he said. "Terry is just too stubbornly in love with her to know it."

At least someone around here is in love with something.

"That, and it's still one of the only four working vehicles we have around here," he added.

"Barely," I commented.

"Devotion counts for a lot," he said.

I wondered if he was referring to me at all.

I decided to come right out and ask him. "How long were you thinking about this?"

He turned and grinned at me. "Longer than you probably think," he said. "I didn't choose you lightly, Evelyn. I honestly decided you were the best choice, and that was after a lot of consideration, believe me."

I wasn't overly encouraged. It sounded like he was thinking of me like a new car that he'd bought.

As I contemplated what to say next, I turned my head to the sound of running feet and panting breath approaching. Three lupine shapes came bounding up to us, whom I was able to identify by their scents as Marla, Ken and Rudy.

I also noticed that Ken was sporting a deep, nasty bite in his shoulder, which became more obvious when the three of them shifted to their two-legged forms, and the fur that partially obscured the wound disappeared. They looked haggard and exhausted, Ken especially. I could smell the faint aroma of a strange wolf on him.

"What happened?" Leon said.

"The Morgandorf Pack," Rudy said through heavy breaths. "They're getting bolder. We ran into four of them on the wrong side of our western border. When we tried to chase them out they attacked us, as if they didn't care they were in our territory. Ken got it good."

Leon's face looked grim. "Where did they go?"

"After they took a bite out of Ken, we tried to chase them off," Marla said. "We were outnumbered, though. They stood their ground, but then decided to slink back where they came from before things got too ugly."

"This won't be the end of it," Leon said. "If the Morgandorfs are disregarding our borders and not even trying to hide it, we can expect them to show up again, in numbers this time." He looked over the trio and said, "Ken, go get that looked at. The rest of you get cleaned up, and tell everyone to gather tonight for a howl."

They all nodded, and headed off. Leon's calm smirk was gone, replaced by that narrow-eyed look of venom he always got whenever the subject of the Morgandorfs came up. He wasn't alone, either. Many members of my pack seemed to know only one way to say that name, and that was by spitting it out as if it were a curse. Dad in particular had always been especially vehement in referring to our neighboring pack.

"Are you planning something?" I asked him with more than a little concern.

He turned to me again, still not regaining his confident look. "Nothing drastic, don't worry. But we do need to prepare ourselves for the possibility of those Morgandorf fleabags trying to move in on us. Consider this a yellow alert."

Again, I wasn't encouraged.

Then suddenly his smirk returned with a vengeance, and he put a hand on my shoulder. "You'll be by my side when I address the pack tonight," he said. "You should get a taste of being my pack mistress. I think you will learn to like it. Even if it is in time of conflict."

I didn't say anything. It seemed like whatever I had to say would not have mattered. He obviously had everything figured out.

"I promise you, once you're up on that rock by my side, with everyone in the pack bowing to you, you'll feel the power. And you'll never want to let it go."

Then he just walked away, not even waiting for a response from me. I sighed. That didn't go the way I wanted at all.

<u>CHAPTER TWO</u>

I always loved the howls, gathering with the whole pack under the moon and stars, howling to the sky with the crackling bonfire lighting up the night. I loved getting pumped up as our alpha led the cheer, while I hooted and hollered along with everyone around me. I loved when we all started stripping our clothes off, and then shifting into our four-legged shapes to continue the howl. And I loved running off into the woods, feeling the wind in my fur, and finding some large animal to bring down, or else finding some random packmate to hook up with, where we would shift back to our two-legged forms and fuck in the dirt.

But that was before I was engaged to the alpha of our pack.

That night, I stood beside him on the big rock, looking down at all the friends and family I'd known my whole life. The whole situation felt wrong. I belonged down there, among my pack brothers and sisters, not standing up on a pedestal above them. Looking down, I saw them all becoming riled and excited. Any other night I would've been right there with them, getting my blood pumping just as they were.

Tonight I felt no excitement.

Leon stepped forward, looking down over the pack. "My brothers and sisters of the Caldour Pack!" he called. "We stand on lands that have been ours for generations! Every rock, every tree, every blade of grass on this land, we are the rulers of it all! Our ancestors, our mothers and fathers ruled it just as we do, and I say to you that our children will rule it just as we have!"

The pack shouted and pumped their fists.

"But," he went on, "we must not drop our guard. There are those who would take everything we love from us, and if we grow complacent, they will succeed. Our neighbors from the Morgandorf Pack have seen fit to disregard our borders. They have crossed into our territory and taken our game, and if we let them, they will surely take our homes too!"

A chorus of canine barks and growls arose from the pack.

"But we will not let them!" Leon shouted as various pack members began shedding their clothes. "We will make our stand here! We will not let a single Morgandorf cross our borders, or take what is ours! And every creature that walks, flies or crawls will know, we are the strongest beasts in these lands! We will make sure none of them will dare to challenge us again!"

Articles of clothing dropped like snowflakes as the pack erupted in howls. Leon joined them all, throwing his head back and howling to the sky, as the pack followed along with him. One by one, members of the pack began dropping to the ground, shifting to their four-legged shapes and filling the night with their eerie song.

Finally, Leon started to join them, throwing off his leather jacket and stripping away his shirt, revealing the many scars that covered his torso. Scars were not uncommon among our pack; as I said before, many wolves obtained scars from fighting in the ring.

Most of Leon's scars weren't from the fights. At least not from fights with members of his own pack.

Most of them were courtesy of the Morgandorfs.

Just like my dad's scars.

Leon had a lot of personal bad blood with our neighboring pack. He'd pretty much been born into our ongoing feud with them, and had carried it on like the dutiful alpha he was. Of course, I'd only ever heard about these supposed boogeymen who lived a few miles outside our territory, never having encountered them myself. I never understood what it was we had against them. I was always told they were the enemy.

Leon turned to me as he started unfastening his pants. "Waiting for something?" he said. "You're an example to them now. You ought to act like one of them."

I was *one of them,* I thought as he shifted to his four-legged form. When I realized I was the only one still two-legged, I decided I might as well follow along. I sighed, and off came my clothes. I dropped forward onto all fours as my fur sprouted and my face reshaped into a wolf's snout. But even then, I didn't find myself joining the howl.

Well, at least not at first. For a while, Leon led the pack in howling , while I simply sat beside him, idle. Finally, I realized I was just being obstinate, and let myself join. Leon howled again, and I finally threw my head back and let the night hear my song.

As they always did, the pack soon scattered, running off into the woods. This time I didn't hesitate to join them. This was exactly what I wanted to do, more than anything. I wanted to run. I wanted to run far away, if I could. The only thing that was different about this than it was on any other howl we'd had was that I didn't want to run alongside the rest of the pack.

I wanted to run alone.

As we hurried down off the rock and followed the pack disappearing into the trees, I stayed at Leon's side just as long as I had to. I wasn't sure if he would try to follow me if I tried to go my own way, but I felt it was worth trying. Besides, it wasn't like I was trying to escape from him or anything; I just needed some freedom and solitude.

Soon enough, however, the issue got resolved for me as we caught the scent of a deer. Immediately the whole pack went charging in that direction. No one noticed when I decided to go off on my own. I peeled away from Leon's side as he joined the others closing in on their new found quarry, and I dashed off into the brush.

Thankfully, I neither heard nor smelled anyone following after me. I was free to run where I wanted for now. I raced away from all the pressures of my pack's expectations. I raced away from the pressures of my alpha wanting me to be his. I raced away from the pressures of my father having my life already planned out for me.

I'm not sure how long I ran. It was like I intended to keep running until I felt like I'd left all my worries behind, even though I knew I could never run far enough for that. I finally stopped by a creek, where I caught my breath for a minute, and lowered my head to lap up a drink of water.

I allowed myself a moment to forget everything. I even let myself forget that there was anything human about me. As far as I was concerned, at that moment, I was just a wolf out in nature, enjoying the stillness of the woods and the cool water soothing my parched throat after a good run. I let myself forget that I had an alpha, or even a pack. I allowed myself a moment to believe there was only me.

That is until I heard something move.

I lifted my head, moving my ears about and sniffing the air. At first, I detected nothing. Maybe it had just been a raccoon or something that had scurried away. I wasn't hungry enough to go after it.

Suddenly, I looked around me, and realized I no longer knew where I was. I'd never run this far before; could I have crossed outside of Caldour territory? I'd never even been beyond the borders of my pack's hunting grounds. For a second I started to worry that I might not be able to find my way back… but then, my own scent trail couldn't be too hard to follow, could it? I couldn't have gone *that* far. I'd be able to find the scents of my pack soon enough; I was sure of it.

Just then I caught another scent.

Whatever it was that had moved before, moved again, and this time the wind brought its scent to me. The scent was unmistakable.

Wolf.

And not just any wolf.

A wolf like me.

A shifter.

And it wasn't from my pack.

I tensed up, searching about for the strange wolf I smelled. I even dared him to show himself, giving a soft but sharp *"huff!"*

Finally, a head emerged from around a tree, cautiously moving forward, sniffing the air coming off me. We spent a moment simply standing there, tensed, regarding each other. So far, I could tell only that he was a he, and that he was not of the Caldour Pack. Anything beyond that could only be conjecture.

At least until he finally decided to take a chance on me and shifted to his two-legged form. A lean, light haired man in his mid-twenties suddenly stood in the place of the wolf that had been there a few seconds before, looking down at me cautiously. It was obviously a risky move; in my four-legged form, I could easily rip him to shreds, so he was effectively dropping his guard. I decided to take that as a show of faith.

So I shifted back to my two-legged form as well. "Who are you?" I demanded.

"A little forward, aren't you?" he said. "You're the one who's on my turf; who are you?"

"Why should I tell you who I am?"

"I could say the same. We could go back and forth like this all night, if you want."

My lip curled up. "Are you a Morgandorf?"

"You're in Morgandorf territory, or didn't you know that?" he said. "Were you looking for us?"

I didn't have a sharp retort ready. "No," I said. "I was just running. I was getting away from my pack. I guess I got lost."

"Getting away from your pack?" he said. "Why, what'd they do to you?"

"It's none of your business!" I snapped.

"It is if you're in our territory," he said. "Were you looking for a new pack, then?"

"Never!" I declared. "I wasn't running away. I just wanted to get away for a bit."

He nodded in understanding, but still watched me suspiciously. "This pack of yours... that wouldn't be the Caldour Pack, would it?"

I cautiously took a step back. This had the potential to get really ugly really quick. "What if it is?" I asked. "Will you turn me over to your alpha, and have them pass sentence on me?"

"Why should I want to do that?" he said. "Have you done something to us that needs to be punished? 'Cause as far as I can tell, all you did was get a little water from one of our creeks. Call me crazy, but that doesn't seem like much of an offense to me."

For a moment, I didn't say anything. "So what *do* you want with me?"

He shrugged. "I just wanted to know why you're here. That's all."

"So… you're gonna let me go back to my pack now?"

"Do you want to?" he asked. "You're the one who said you were trying to get away from them."

I didn't say anything then.

"What were you trying to get away from?" he finally asked.

I wasn't sure why, but I felt comfortable enough now to open up a little more.
"My alpha wants me to marry him."

He nodded. "And you're not too keen on the idea?"

"I don't know what I am on it."

"But you say you're not running away?"

"Everyone I know is there," I said. "My family, my friends… I don't know anyone outside my pack. Besides, I'm not *totally* opposed to marrying him."

"But you're opposed a little, aren't you?" he said. "Or else you wouldn't be this far from them."

I couldn't argue with that.

"What are you going to do?" he asked me. "Will you go back to them?"

"I can't imagine I won't," I replied. "Why, are you offering to set me up with your pack?"

He tilted his head and studied me. "I don't recall saying anything like that. But that's interesting, that your mind went there."

"Well, I mean… I wasn't suggesting…"

"Don't stress about it," he said, putting his hands forward in a calming gesture. "I don't think accepting a Caldour among us would go over well even if you were asking."

"Well that's fine, because I wasn't. I love my pack. They're everything to me."

"But your alpha isn't, is he? You say you don't want to leave your pack, but you obviously don't want to be with them right now. I can't take you to mine either. So where does that leave you?"

I paused to think of an answer—and I really did not have one. "Nowhere, I guess."

He shrugged, and gestured to the ground beneath my feet. "Right here seems like a good enough place. I'm here, if you need someone to listen."

Suddenly I wasn't sure what to make of the man in front of me. "What's your name?" I asked him.

"Jeremy," he said. "Yours?"

Hesitantly I answered, "Evelyn."

"That's pretty," he said. The step he took then was the first time I actually noticed him moving closer to me. It was only at that point that I realized he had been slowly coming closer to me the whole time.

A howl rang out in the distance behind me. Immediately I recognized the voice. It was Leon calling for me. "Oh shit, that's my alpha," I said. "I've got to go!"

He shrugged. "All right. If that's where you really want to be… I'll leave you to him." He turned around to start walking away. "Who am I to stand in your way?"

"Wait!" I said, holding a hand out to him. He turned to look at me… and I paused, not certain I really should say what I wanted to him. After a few seconds, say it I did.

"Can I see you again?"

His mouth curled into a smile. "I don't see why not, if you don't. Come back here tomorrow night?"

"I can sneak out after midnight," I offered.

"Works for me."

Almost against my own volition, I caught a smile cracking across my face.

"See you then," he said, before shifting to his four-legged form and loping off into the brush.

I stood there staring after him, until I heard Leon call for me again. I came back to reality then, and turned and shifted back to my four-legged form to go rejoin my pack.

*

Most of the pack was just getting back to the village by the time I returned. My pack brothers and sisters were returning to their two-legged shapes and busily retrieving their clothes when I emerged from the trees.

Leon had already redressed when I found him, and he stepped up to me. "There you are!" he said. "Where did you disappear to?"

I shifted to my two-legged form again, and carefully met his gaze. "Well, I… I just…. ran off somewhere else. I got a little lost and… had to find my way back."

After I met a Morgandorf wolf and agreed to meet him again tomorrow. Yeah, things wouldn't be pretty if he knew that part.

"Why didn't you join us for the hunt?" he asked. "This was our first howl with you as my betrothed, and you were nowhere to be found!"

I wondered if he could sense my nervousness. "I just wasn't hungry for deer," I shrugged.

He cocked his head, studying me. I bit my lip, unable to guess what he was thinking. "All right then," he said, "what are you hungry for?"

"What?"

"If you're going to be my wife, I have to make sure you're taken care of, and that means keeping you fed, don't you think? I have plenty of food to offer you. It's the least I can do."

"Um… thanks, but I'm not really hungry now." I started walking past him to find my clothes.

Leon reached out and took hold of my arm to stop me. "Oh, don't be coy," he said. "You have to eat something. The last thing I want is for you to starve yourself out of jitters."

As lightly as I could, I pushed his hand away from my arm. "Really, it's okay. I'll get something to eat at home, don't worry about me."

When I again attempted to go for my clothes, he suddenly moved in front of me, blocking my path. "Is there something wrong? You seem bothered."

Well, he wasn't wrong, especially at that point. I was beginning to lose my patience with him. "I just want to be alone right now," I finally said. "Please."

This time when I went to retrieve my clothes, he didn't try to stop me. I got dressed and headed back to my house without a backward glance at him.

Mom and Dad weren't back yet when I got home. That was fine by me. I had meant what I said to Leon out there; I really did want to be alone at that time. There was no one that I could really talk to, not about what had happened tonight. If even one person learned I'd spoken to a Morgandorf... I didn't even want to think about it.

I also meant what I said when I'd told him I'd get something to eat at home. I actually was a little hungrier than I'd let on; I just wasn't interested in being fed by him. I found a can of ravioli in the cupboard, which I didn't even bother to heat up. I just opened it, grabbed a fork and started munching it out of the can.

My parents returned shortly after that, coming in the door just as I was tossing the empty can away. "Evelyn?" my mother called as they came in.

I sighed. "In here," I called from the kitchen.

As they appeared out of the entryway, Dad quickly made a beeline for me. "Leon tells me you gave him a bit of the cold shoulder tonight," he said.

I rolled my eyes. Not more of this!

"I didn't give him the cold shoulder," I protested. "He was just kind of pestering me a little."

"*Pestering?*" Dad gasped, seemingly taken aback by that word. "Don't you think your alpha and future husband is due a little more respect than that?"

"I have nothing but respect for Leon," I said. "I just didn't want to be bothered. I have that right, don't I?"

"Of course you do, dear," Mom nodded, putting a hand on my shoulder. "She does, doesn't she?" she said to Dad.

Dad swallowed his indignation, rolling his eyes and giving a subtle nod. "Yes, yes, you do," he sighed. "But I really have to say, your whole attitude since Leon made his declaration yesterday has been bothering me. This is the greatest thing that's ever happened to you, and you've been acting like you've received a prison sentence!"

Maybe I have, I thought.

I did not give him a verbal answer, though. I walked by him, heading for my room. "I think I'm gonna go to bed."

"Evelyn!" my dad called. "Evelyn, come back here!"

Mom intervened, stepping in between Dad and me as I walked away. "Rene, leave her alone."

I didn't see the rest of the exchange, stepping through my bedroom door and shutting it behind me. I collapsed onto my bed, where I was safe, comfortable, and alone. There was no one in the room to harass me, to pressure me into anything. There was no one there, who made it necessary for me hide my feelings. I was still trying to get my head around it. Tonight I had spoken to an enemy. And I had asked to do it again.

Was he really an enemy? He didn't seem like one. He was just *supposed* to be an enemy; because he was a Morgandorf, he bore the label. But tonight I'd been able to open up with him like I hadn't been able to with anyone, even my own pack.

Well, maybe Charlene. A little.

The point was, the man I met tonight had in no way resembled the bloodthirsty savages and marauders I'd heard about all my life. He didn't act like he was trying to steal land or game from me. If he'd wanted to steal me away from my pack, he'd had the perfect opportunity to do it, and he didn't.

Instead, he'd seemed concerned with nothing more than my well-being. Nothing about him had said "enemy" to me.

Could I really be betraying my whole pack by opening up to a guy like that?

No, I firmly decided then. I was not. Just because my pack wouldn't have approved didn't mean I was betraying them.

Besides, the pack seemed to think they needed to make all my life choices for me. This one choice I could make for myself. If I wanted to see Jeremy again, I would, and everyone would just have to stay out of my way.

*

I didn't know whether to be relieved or insulted at how little attention anyone seemed to pay to me the next day. It was like the whole buzz about me becoming the alpha's betrothed had already passed, and now it was on to the next thing.

Even Leon himself barely seemed to notice me. Apparently, the chase was over, if there had ever been one to begin with, which as far as I knew there hadn't been. He had declared me his and that was that; over, done deal. Apparently in his view, that meant he no longer needed to pay me any mind.

While that wasn't overly flattering, it did make things easier for me.

The one person who did have his eyes on me regularly was my dad. All throughout the day, I would keep looking up and finding him watching me, regarding me with his disapproving glare. It was as if he was studying me, trying to figure me out, wondering what was wrong with me. Like, could I really be his daughter?

Thankfully, I did get the occasional reprieve when Dad wasn't around, and I could just talk to someone like Charlene. I met with her for lunch, when we decided to take a little trip into town for some takeout.

"You made any kind of decision about Leon?" she asked me as we sat over our platters of Chinese.

"Not really," I shrugged. "I think I'm more or less in the same place I was when he announced the whole thing."

"Cause, you know, if you don't want him, I'll take him off your hands!" she smirked.

I wasn't entirely sure if she was being facetious or not. It might simplify things if she could really do that, which made it that much more unfortunate that Leon had more than likely irrevocably made up his mind.

So, instead of answering, I just chewed on a mouthful of sweet-and-sour chicken.

"Come on, lighten up," she said. "You could be way worse off."

"Yeah, I could," I lamented. "But I still wish it didn't feel like my life was being lived for me."

There was a brief pause, before Charlene finally said, "You know, you could always say no. Leon and your dad won't like it, but you could still do it."

"I know I could," I admitted. "I just don't think I'm prepared for the fallout. Right now, I'm just trying to see if there's another way."

"Another way? Like what?"

I grimaced. "I'll let you know when I figure it out."

Maybe I wanted to see Jeremy again out of a desire to find the answer.

I still didn't want to mention him to Charlene, either. I trusted her, but I doubted that even she would respond well to the idea of me meeting with a Morgandorf.

Getting out of the house that night was not the easiest task to pull off. Not with the way Dad was always on my case, bothering me to accept that what was happening was the best thing for me. I eventually excused myself to my room, and waited for Mom and Dad to go to sleep. This, of course, meant waiting a long time with my ear against the door.

Finally, a little while before midnight I started to pick up the sound of Dad snoring. As soon as I heard that, I slipped across the room, slithered out of my clothes and climbed through the window, shifting to my four-legged shape as I leaped to the ground below.

I ran hard into the dark woods ahead of me. I rushed through the trees, stirring the animals that slept in them, and scattering the ones that were still moving. The forest was nearly pitch dark at this hour, but it wasn't important. I didn't need to see where I was going.

My wolf's nose knew the scents of the forest, the smells of dirt and leaves and grass, and knew just where all of it was. My wolf's ears could hear every rustle of the brush, every owl's hoot, every critter scurrying away. My wolf's paws could feel the earth under them, every rock and ditch that I crossed, and I pushed off it all, driving myself forward.

For a minute or so, I worried I wouldn't be able to find the spot again; after all, I'd been running kind of aimlessly when I found him the first time. I'd tried to make it a point on my way back to learn the trail, to recognize the sounds and scents to lead me back there. Soon enough, I stepped out into the area just barely illuminated by the sliver of moonlight streaming through, bouncing off the trickling creek.

I lifted my head and sniffed the air, searching about for the scent of the strange wolf I had met last night. At first, I smelled nothing, and I began to worry he might not show. Then the wind blew in just the right direction, and I turned my head as that distinct scent reached my nose. I hurried forward a few steps, before I shifted back to two legs.

"Jeremy?" I called into the darkness.

"I'm here," his voice called back.

I saw movement within the gloom, and into the minimal light, his figure emerged. Any creature with duller senses than mine would never have been able to tell it was he. But my wolf senses immediately recognized the mysterious stranger from last night.

"I was worried I wouldn't find you," I said.

"Really? Did you have trouble getting away?"

"Not once my father went to bed," I said. "I had to wait a long time for that, though."

He smirked slightly. "Sneaking out your bedroom window," he mused. "Is that a normal thing for you?"

I shook my head. "No. I've never done anything like this before. I've always been daddy's girl."

"Don't tell me that all changed because of me?"

"No, it's not all you," I said, shaking my head again. "I think it's because of this whole marriage arrangement. Dad wants me to marry the alpha so that he can have alpha grandkids."

"And the question of what you want isn't even on the table?" he said.

"Something like that," I said.

"Have you told anyone else how you feel about this?"

"Most of the she-wolves in my pack are so jealous of me, I don't think they'd believe me if I said I don't want to marry Leon. There's one friend I have who I can kind of talk to, but even she thinks I should just get over myself and realize I'm the luckiest girl in the pack."

"So no one really gets you, do they?" he said.

I looked up at him. *I think you do,* I thought. I didn't feel comfortable enough to say that out loud.

"Why are you so interested in me?" I suddenly asked. "Is this a charity case, or are you trying to get inside info?"

His face fell. "You still think I'm trying to take advantage of you? Just because you're a Caldour?"

I shrugged. "I've got to at least consider it, don't I? I mean you seem like a nice guy, but… you're still a Morgandorf. And I've never heard any good things about the Morgandorfs."

"I've never heard any good things about the Caldours, either," he said. "But here we are. And as I recall, you were the one who asked to meet again."

I sighed. "Okay, I'm sorry. Forget I said that. But I ask again, why are you so interested in me?"

He shrugged. "Maybe I just find you interesting. Is that so incredible?"

I eyed him suspiciously. "Come on, there's got to be more to it than that."

"Why? What's so uninteresting about you? Your desire to be independent? Your struggle with not being allowed to be? The fact that you have to wander off into the middle of nowhere and unload on a stranger from another pack? Which, by the way, I'm honored to be the one you feel comfortable enough to open up with, especially when you say you can't even do that with anyone from your own pack."

He paused for an instant and then added, "You know, maybe that's what it is. I just like the feeling of being a friendly ear, and you seem like you need one."

For a minute, I didn't say anything more. When I finally did it was a simple, pathetic, "Oh. Okay."

He reached out a hand and touched my arm. "Tell you what: why don't we go hunt something together? Isn't that the best kind of bonding experience two wolves can have?"

I cocked my head, looking at him with a curious grin. "You want to… bond… with me?"

"Don't you?" he said. "Or at least with somebody?"

I grinned wide enough to show my pearly whites. "After you."

He shook his head, and gestured forward. "Ladies first."

I smiled at him a few seconds longer, and then ran a couple steps forward before shifting into my four-legged form and dashing off into the woods. I almost immediately could hear his paws running behind me, his breath panting as he ran and his claws gripping the dirt beneath him to propel him forward, just as mine were doing.

As I let him catch up to me, I spared a sideways glance to see his lupine form dashing through the dark forest beside me. I realized this was a much different run from the one I took with Charlene the other night. That had been a run to try to get away from my life, to escape the pressures that I was feeling. I just happened to have a friend along with me. Right now, I was already away from my troubles. That was why I had come out here to see Jeremy in the first place, I realized. He had no expectations of me; there were no demands on me with him. For right now, I had no need to escape.

So this was about something else entirely.

We were running to feel alive.

I wasn't unaccustomed to this feeling. Hell, it was how I always used to feel when I took off running after a howl. That was what it was about when everyone in the pack took off into the woods to find whatever we could kill and eat.

Right now, there was no pack running beside me.

There was just him.

Eventually I caught the scent of a rabbit somewhere in the brush. I immediately veered off the trail in its direction, with Jeremy following close at my side. We closed in on the small creature as one, clamping my jaws onto its neck before it even knew we were on it, while Jeremy's teeth sank into its meaty haunches.

As one, we shared in our meal of the small animal. This was the first time in days I didn't feel like I was forcing myself to eat something, or seeking comfort food. I honestly felt there was no place I would have rather been.

I gulped down the rabbit meat and licked my chops, and then looked at Jeremy as he lifted his head from our kill. I moved forward, nuzzling my snout against his, making a happy little whine. When I felt him nuzzling me back, I knew my advances weren't unwarranted.

So, that was when I went for broke.

I *pounced* on him, tumbling with him to the ground as we rubbed our noses together. As we rolled about in the dirt, as one, we suddenly shifted to our two-legged forms, finding ourselves entangled in a naked heap on the ground, with our faces just inches apart.

I closed that distance.

I kissed him deep, deeper than I could ever remember kissing anyone before. I felt his hand come up and grip the back of my head, entangling in my hair, while his other hand stroked along my spine.

When I lifted my head and looked down at him, he said, "You're pretty forward, aren't you?"

"It just felt like the thing to do," I said. "You're not complaining, are you?"

"Not for a second."

With that out of the way, I kissed him again. I heard myself moaning into his mouth as I fidgeted around on top of him. I ground my pelvis against him, feeling his manhood hardening beneath me, and my loins began to moisten in response. His hand came down to cup the curve of my ass, making goose bumps break out across my skin.

He rolled us over, putting himself on top, and ducked his head to capture my tit in his mouth. I rolled my head back and arched my chest upward, pushing more of my breast into his mouth. His hand meanwhile slid down my belly, coming to the junction of my legs where my wetness awaited him. His fingers ducked inside me, making my hips leap up off the ground as I gasped sharply, grabbing him by the wrist. He slowly began pumping his fingers inside me, his thumb diddling my clit, playing me like a musical instrument. It was certainly making some kind of music come out of me.

By the time I felt my juices trickling down my ass, I was worked up beyond the point of waiting any longer. I reached down and grabbed the stiff tool that jutted from his loins, stroking it in my hand. "Put it in me, please!" I begged.

He didn't disappoint me. He maneuvered himself between my spread legs, and down he plunged.

My head lolled to the side, letting out a loud groan as he parted my nether lips. He slowly began working his way into me, one thrust at a time. He got an inch or two in on the first thrust, and got progressively deeper, bottoming out on about thrust number five. At that point, my hands came up to wrap around his shoulders, embracing him to me as he proceeded thrusting inside me.

Most of the times I would hook up with guys before had been just random, casual encounters after a howl. It usually was about nothing more than the excitement of the moment, and the thought that went into choosing a partner had rarely been more complicated than who was nearest to me when the mood struck. It was just how a pack typically lived; socialize normally with them most of the time, but during a howl, inhibitions went out the window, and everyone could be as promiscuous as they wanted.

There had been a few guys over the years whom I'd been with outside of the howls, but none of them had ever been serious. It was always just about "scratching each other's itch," so to speak. I honestly couldn't remember a time I'd hooked up with someone when my choice of partner had been anything other than just convenient.

This was nothing like that. This wasn't a case of me simply wanting to be fucked. I wanted to be fucked by *him*. I wanted *Jeremy*.

With that in mind, I clutched his body that much tighter, wanting to envelop him whole. My legs came up, hugging his hips and wrapping about him as I tried to urge him on. My mouth hung open as he gradually sped up his thrusting, driving me to greater heights of pleasure. My pelvis moved up to meet his thrusts, rubbing my clit along his pelvic bone.

I rode the wave of mounting sensation in my loins, coming steadily closer to something I had never achieved just from straight fucking before. When I realized he was getting close to making me climax, it only made me that much more excited, and only served to get me even closer. "Oh god," I gasped, "I think I'm gonna cum! Fuck me faster!"

He responded by speeding up just as I asked him to, and I felt my impending orgasm coming closer. I let it come, welcoming it with open arms, letting it take me over.

When it finally came, I let loose, thrashing my body beneath his weight, screaming to the night sky. I think I heard the leaves rustling about me as the creatures in the trees fled from the sound of my cries, but I was so delirious at that point, it was hard to be sure.

When I came down from my high and regained my senses, Jeremy was still thrusting.

I suddenly held up a hand to stop him. "Wait, stop, I need a minute," I said. I was a bit too sensitive after my orgasm to continue right away. He sat up and pulled out of me, exposing his glistening wet cock to the moonlight. I bent forward, slurping him into my mouth, tasting the tangy flavor of myself on him. My head bobbed back and forth on his pole, my cheeks caving in around him, sucking him voraciously. I heard a grunt of appreciation come from him, and I felt his hand running through my hair.

When I felt I'd given my pussy enough of a break, I got up and turned over on my hands and knees, putting my ass upright in his direction. He took hold of my hips, stroking the curve of my ass as he positioned himself behind me. He slotted his cock in my opening and pushed forward, burying himself in a single thrust this time. I grunted hard, digging my fingers into the dirt.

He started to build up a rhythm as he thrust into me from behind, his hips repeatedly slapping against my ass. I soon dropped to my elbows, my eyes shut and my mouth open as one pleasured grunt after another escaped my mouth.

He bent forward, pressing himself to the length of my back, and moving his hands from my hips to my swaying breasts. He squeezed them in his powerful hands, kneading the soft flesh and playing my stiff nipples, sending further shivers of excitement through me.

With his added stimulation on my tits combined with his continued thrusting, I soon found myself soaring through my second orgasm of the night, and my second ever from simple thrusting. It wasn't as intense as the first, but it still made me collapse forward, screaming into the dirt. And after he did that, he thrust forward once more and held himself there, grunting behind me as I felt him splashing against my insides.

For a long while, neither of us moved. I lay there with my face in the dirt while he held himself inside me, both of us catching our breath. Eventually, he withdrew his softening cock and came down to the ground with me, and I reached out an arm for him, pulling myself to his body and resting my head against his chest.

"You're all glowy," he murmured above my head.

I raised my head to look at his face, barely visible in the moonlight. "How can you even tell? It's dark as pitch here."

"There's plenty of light coming from you," he said. "I take it that was good for you, too?"

He was right; I couldn't stop smiling. "Yeah. Don't let this inflate your ego too much, but that was the best I've ever had. I've never actually cum during sex before. Every orgasm I've ever had has been either self-induced or from someone eating me out."

"Maybe you just weren't with the right partners," he said. He paused a moment, and then suddenly asked, "By chance, does that include your alpha?"

I shook my head. "No. I've never done it with Leon."

As soon as his name escaped my mouth, the reality of what had just happened came crashing in, and I sat bolt upright. "Oh my god! Leon! Oh, shit, what did I just do?"

"What you wanted, didn't you?" he said, sitting up more slowly and putting an arm around my shoulders.

"Yes, but… oh, god, what if they find out about this?"

"You're not planning to tell them, are you?"

I looked down at myself, and held an arm up to my nose and took a sniff. "As soon as they get a whiff of me, I won't have to! I've got your scent all over me!"

Jeremy lifted his head and scanned about, searching the sounds of the forest. "I think I hear the creek off in that direction. Come on, let's go wash."

He rose to his feet with a grunt, and then lowered a hand to help me to my feet. He led me by the hand through the woods until we came to the trickling creek, where I let go of his hand and rushed in. The water was numbingly freezing as I squatted down and splashed it all over myself, rubbing as if my life depended on it, but it was a small price to pay. All I could think of was what Dad would do if he knew what had just happened. Or what Leon would do. A little cold water was nothing compared to that nightmare.

I heard more splashing, and looked to my right to see Jeremy doing the same thing I was. "You don't want my scent either?"

"You think you're the only one who might get in trouble for this?" he said. "I can't go back smelling like a Caldour any more than you can go back smelling like a Morgandorf."

I scrubbed myself until I was certain no one would be able to identify the scent of another wolf on me, and then stepped out of the water and shook myself off. Jeremy stepped up beside me. I looked at him.

I just looked.

I knew I had to go back. I had to.

And it was the hardest thing in the world to tear myself away from the man before me.

"You should be going now," he said.

"I know."

"I should be too," he said.

"You should."

"We ought to be saying goodnight now."

"You're absolutely right."

We waited a few seconds more before temptation overtook us. And then we *launched* ourselves at each other for the most intense goodnight kiss I'd ever had. It was like we were trying to *devour* each other, our mouths pressed together so hard. Our tongues seemed to be trying to tie themselves into a knot with the way they danced together, and our hands couldn't seem to find any one part of each other they wanted to grab onto, with the way they kept moving all over each other's bodies.

It was he who finally broke the kiss, suddenly turning four-legged and scampering off into the dark woods. As he disappeared into the brush, I paused, needing to catch my breath again after the intensity of that.

Just before I was about to turn to leave, I happened to sniff myself one more time. *Oh, great, now I've got to wash again.*

CHAPTER THREE

Well, it was now official. I had slept with the enemy. I was a traitor to my own pack.

At least that was what anyone would say if they found out about this. But it wasn't how I felt.

I actually felt better than I had in weeks.

It was still before dawn when I returned to the village. I scampered through the houses on four paws, hoping no one was awake yet, which they shouldn't have been. I got back to my house and leaped into my open bedroom window, shifting back to two legs once I was inside. When I listened to the sounds of the house, I could hear Dad still snoring. That was good. Still, I gave myself another sniff… and while I was pretty sure I had gotten most of Jeremy's scent off me, I wanted to be completely sure. Dad probably wouldn't wake up if I took a shower now, would he?

I decided to risk it. If nothing else, it was much nicer getting hot water to wash myself with as opposed to that ice-cold creek, and I didn't have body wash out there in the woods.

Once I was thoroughly cleaned off, I strained my ears again, relieved to hear Dad still snoring. I decided I had best get some sleep while it was still dark, not wanting to appear dead on my feet to the pack during the day tomorrow. I quietly slipped back to my room and curled up in my bed, drifting off to sleep with a happy smile on my face.

Unsurprisingly, Mom and Dad were already up when I awoke. It was the smell of Mom's cooking that roused me, and I quickly threw on some light clothes and walked out of my room with my best morning face on.

"Morning, Mom. Morning Daddy!" I chirped as I stepped out into the kitchen.

Dad looked up from his plate of bacon and eggs, and cocked his head. "Well good morning, sweetheart. You look chipper this morning."

"Do I?" I said, trying to appear as innocent as possible. "I don't feel any different." I sat down at the counter next to Dad, and looked to Mom preparing a plate for me. "Mm, that smells good, Mom!"

"Would you like some jam on your toast, Evie?"

"Yes please. Strawberry, if we have any."

As Mom went to put the finishing touches on my breakfast, I felt Dad staring at me. I turned my head to see him studying me with a tilted head. I suddenly started to grow nervous. Could he tell? Was he suspicious? Was I acting too innocent?

As I watched him, a bright smile slowly spread across his face. I tried not to bite my lip out of anxiety. "You're finally warming up to it, aren't you?"

"What?"

"Leon. Your engagement to him. Becoming the wife of the alpha. You're finally starting to like the idea, aren't you?"

I put on a smile that was half-fake, half-relieved. "Uh, yeah! You figured me out, Dad! I'm just giddy with the idea! I think it's—"

"Aren't you going to eat?" Mom said.

I looked down to see the plate of food set in front of me that I had not even noticed before. "Oh, yes, thanks Mom," I said as I dug in, eating a little too fast. I slowed down as I felt eyes on me, carefully chewing the bite of toast I had in my mouth. I had to be more careful not to be so obvious. That was the kind of thing that would surely give me away…

"What's that smell?"

I nearly choked a chill running through me when Dad said that. I looked up at him, wide-eyed. Had I missed something? I scrubbed myself three times, didn't I? Was that not enough? How did he…?

"Something burning?" he said.

Mom turned around to see the eggs that were still on the skillet starting to smoke. "Ah!" she gasped, rushing to the stove and picking up the skillet to turn the eggs over. "Well, I hope no one wanted seconds," she said.

I breathed a huge—but subdued—breath of relief, and went back to quietly eating. That had most likely taken years off my life.

I got through the rest of my meal pretty uneventfully, other than Dad stepping out a little early to go tell Leon the "good news." *Wonderful,* I thought. Like I needed this scenario to get any more complicated.

When I was finished, I changed into something a little more presentable and walked out of the house, finding the rest of the pack up and about, going about their day.

As I walked among them, a part of me could not help but feel a bit like an outsider. They were my pack; they always had been. I had grown up among them all. They had always been part of my life. Yet, if a single one of them knew who I had been with last night, I knew they would have cast me out in an instant. Was that loyalty? Or was it that I had forgone my own loyalty? That was how they would have spun it.

When it came right down to it, could I really even call myself one of them anymore?

Eventually, Charlene found me, moving to intercept me as I passed the circle where she and a few others sat around chatting about whatever. "Hey, Evie," she said—and then looked me over. "You look different."

No I don't. Don't tell me I look different. I am just the same as always. Nothing's changed. Please don't say anything is different.

"I don't feel any different," I said, echoing my words to Dad earlier.

Charlene looked at me suspiciously. "No... there's something..."

She took me by the wrist and led me away from where anyone was around, and then looked at me again. Her eyes widened, and she raised a finger to point at me. Dropping her mouth open, she suddenly gasped, *"YOU HAD SEX!"*

In a rush of panic, I clapped a hand over her mouth, desperately looking around to see if anyone heard her, and put a finger to my lips to shush her.

She pulled my hand from her mouth and laughed. "That was a confirmation if I ever saw one!"

I grimaced. "Tell me it's not that obvious?"

She shook her head and scoffed. "Girl, it's written all over you!"

"No, please! It can't be written all over me! Tell me it's not written all over me!"

She retreated back, a little intimidated. "Well… maybe it's just woman's intuition?"

"Leon can't find out! Neither can my dad! In fact, *no one* can find out!"

"Okay, okay!" she insisted. "My lips are sealed!" Then she looked around, and leaned forward before saying in a conspiratorial whisper, "But you gotta tell me who!"

"No!" I declared, shaking my head. "I'm not saying another word!"

"Come on, it's me! Was it Tucker?"

"No, it wasn't Tucker."

"Well then, was it Alex? You know he had his eye on you for a while before Leon moved in."

"No. It wasn't Alex."

"Joey?"

"Stop guessing! Please!"

"What are you ladies up to?" a voice said, making me nearly jump out of my skin. I turned to find Leon approaching, a proud smile on his face and a pompous swagger in his step.

Thankfully, for as long I'd been wishing for her to stop talking, Charlene did know when it was the right time to button it. "Oh, nothing," she said. "Just girl talk."

"I'm sure," he said. He looked at me directly. "I spoke to your father," he said. "He tells me you might be starting to come around on my proposal."

"Uh… well… Dad might be getting a little overzealous… but…"

"I understand if you're still nervous," he said, putting what I think he meant to be a comforting hand on my shoulder. "The wedding doesn't have to happen too soon if you don't want. We can make it next spring, how about that?"

I just stared back, my mouth kind of hanging open. "Uh… I… uh…"

"Just think about it," he said. "I'm sure it'll seem more real the closer it gets."

With that, he walked away. No waiting for any further response; he had made his decision, and that was just that.

"I hate to say it, but I'm beginning to understand why you're not jumping at the chance to marry him,"

Charlene said. "That was like he thinks you're his PA or something."

I said nothing.

"Evie?"

I still didn't say anything. I just couldn't breathe.

*

"I knew the whole time what it meant," I said as I lay curled up against Jeremy's chest. "But as soon as he said the word 'wedding' I just froze. The thought of marrying him was always just an idea, until he went and made it real. He was talking about it happening next spring. He put an actual time frame on it."

"What did you say to him?" he asked.

"Nothing!" I said. "I just kind of stood there in stunned silence. You know, he didn't even wait for me to say anything! He just said it and walked away, like it was a done deal."

"What are you going to do?" he said.

That was the ultimate question, wasn't it? What *was* I going to do?

I at least knew one thing for certain that I had only been ambivalent about before, I did not want to marry Leon. Not when the idea of it scared me that much.

"I just wish there was some way I could say no to him."

"If you ask me," Jeremy said, "any alpha who would deny you your own life choices doesn't deserve to be your alpha."

"It's not just him that I would be defying," I said. "How do I tell my father I don't want to marry him? There's no way Dad will accept that!"

"So you can't refuse to marry him without going against both your alpha and your dad. So where does that leave you?"

"I wish I knew," I groaned, pulling myself tighter against his body. "I just don't see a way out. Not without running away altogether."

"Would you do that?"

I blinked. I actually wasn't serious when I said that last part, but when Jeremy suggested the idea I stopped to actually consider it. The idea did not seem any less frightening than the idea of marrying Leon. Run away? Abandon everyone I knew? How could I do that? Where would I go?

"Your silence is saying a lot," he said.

I sighed. "I guess this is what they call a rock and a hard place."

"So then… you will marry him?"

I frowned, searching for a way to say no. When I couldn't find one, I shrugged. "Hell, maybe it won't change anything," I sighed. "For a guy who claims to want me for his wife, he barely seems to pay any attention to me. Maybe he won't even notice if we keep this up."

He slipped his hand under my back, cradling me in his arms. "Something tells me you don't really believe that."

"Well, it doesn't matter," I decided. "Whatever he says or does, he can't stop me from seeing you if I want to."

"You sound like you're trying to convince yourself of that more than me."

"Can't you just let me believe it for a while?" I said before giving him a deep kiss.

The load of cum he had already given me tonight sloshed around inside me, dribbling out onto my thighs as I pressed my crotch against him. I started to suckle at his neck as he massaged my breast, pinching my nipple in his fingers. I moaned, pushing my chest into his hand.

I felt him hardening again as I rubbed my slit along the length of his dick, making my pussy hungry for the next round. I rolled onto my back and parted my legs, letting him settle between them and slide easily inside my tunnel, which was still dripping wet from our mixed cum.

My eyes fluttered shut as he thrust forward, filling up my depths. I groaned aloud, my fingers clawing at his shoulder blades. My hips moved up to meet his thrusts, my legs hugging his flanks.

Before long, I rolled us over, putting myself on top. I moved my hips back and forth on his lap, feeling him move inside me as I stared down at his face, illuminated by soft moonlight. When everything in my life seemed to be conspiring against me, determined to take my choices away, Jeremy had become the one thing that I could call truly mine. He was my lover, my secret, my safe place. Leon could call me his all he wanted; he would never truly have me. Not the way Jeremy did.

I was so focused on his face, the pleasures running through me, and the soft sounds we were making, that I am not quite sure how I noticed the sound of something rustling in the bushes when I did. I suddenly stopped moving, looking off in that direction. "Did you hear that?"

"Probably just an animal," Jeremy said.

"Maybe," I conceded. I started sniffing the air anyway.

Yes, after a minute, I did smell an animal.

The kind of animal I smelled was enough to alarm me seriously.

"You smell that?" I said.

This time he nodded. "We're not alone."

Somewhat reluctantly, I slipped off Jeremy's lap and crawled forward on all fours, slowly shifting into my four-legged shape as I moved, sniffing at the bushes. Whatever or whoever was there apparently realized I noticed them, and was trying to retreat. I leaped forward, catching the sight of a furry shape dashing out of the brush and charged after it.

My quarry was fast, sprinting around the trees ahead of us. I knew I couldn't let our observer get away to report what they'd seen, so every time the creature ahead of me turned a corner I cut across, quickly gaining ground. Before long, I was close enough to leap forward and pounce on my quarry, pinning it to the ground.

When I had the intruding wolf pinned to the ground beneath me, that was when I finally got the chance to recognize her scent.

All at once, I shifted back to my two-legged form, recoiling back. "Charlene?" I gasped.

Prone on the ground, she retook her own human shape, staring up at me. "Something you want to tell me?" she said.

"What... what are you doing here?"

"That's what I want to ask you," she said. "I was curious when you wouldn't tell me about your mystery lover. So when I caught you sneaking out, I decided to snoop. So..." She looked past my shoulder as Jeremy stepped up behind me. "You want to tell me who that is?"

"Uh... well...he, uh..."

"I'm Jeremy," he said. "And you are?"

"Really, really interested now," was her reply as she started getting to her feet. "Where'd you dig this guy up?"

"Well... I just sort of ran into him the other night, when I went off on my own, and... well..."

Charlene continued eyeing him suspiciously. She took a couple steps toward him. "I can see the attraction," she said, her voice still carrying a tone of wariness. "But... there's something about him..."

She leaned forward, giving him a couple whiffs. "Wait a minute," she said, sniffing him a few more times. "That scent... I've smelled him somewhere before..."

A moment later, her eyes went wild.

"He's a *MORGANDORF!*" she shouted, her teeth extending into wolf fangs, and her eyes turning yellow. She suddenly lunged forward, her eyes feral and full of rage, her teeth bared as she roared out her bloodlust.

I dashed forward and grabbed her, pulling her back. "Charlene, no!"

"Let me at 'im! I'll bite his junk off!"

"Charlene, please! I need you to calm down!"

She stopped struggling against me and turned her attention to me, her eyes regaining their human shade. "Tell me you're not serious! I know you are not crazy about marrying Leon, but *this?* You are fucking a *Morgandorf?* Are you out of your fucking mind?"

"So what if he's a Morgandorf?" I said. "It's just a name."

Charlene whirled on me. "'Just a name?' Do you know where I know his scent from?" she snarled. "It was two years ago. I was out in the woods with

Corey and Jana; we were watching some of the pups. One of them decided to go chasing a rabbit, and next thing you know all the pups are following him, so we have to chase after them. And then we ran into a Morgandorf gathering party." She pointed a stiff, aggressive finger at Jeremy. "Including that dirt wad.

"They took the rabbit the pups were chasing, and told us to piss off and leave them to it. When one of the pups tried to protest, they threatened to kill the pups if we didn't leave! That's who you're fucking, Evie! The Morgandorfs are pup killers!"

"Excuse me," Jeremy spoke up, "that's not quite how I remember it happening."

"Yeah, I'm sure you're gonna go on about how you were the victims in all this, and our pups were the ones threatening you!" Charlene snarled.

"Now, hold on," he said, holding his hands up. "I remember there being a lot of hostility, but I don't remember anyone threatening the pups. I do recall one of your pack stepping in front of the pups and warning us against harming them, claiming that she'd, and I quote, 'have our livers over a spit with some peppers and collard greens' if we hurt one fur on their backs. Which, I might add, I thought was very unwarranted."

"You can say whatever you want, you maggot-eater! I know exactly what you are! All of your damn pack!"

"I'm not denying some of my packmates that were there that day may have said some unpleasant things," Jeremy said. "And plenty of them will readily accuse the Caldours of a lot of the same things of which you are accusing me. In my experience, high tempers and rationality are like oil and water. And tempers certainly run high whenever our packs happen to meet."

"Oh, you're about to find out, shithead!" Charlene growled, before lunging at him again.

I promptly jumped in her path to hold her back. "Charlene, please!" I cried. "You have to promise me you're not going to say anything about this!"

"You gotta be kidding me!" she gasped. "I'm gonna bring the whole pack down on this clown's ass!"

"Charlene!" I shouted. "Please! For me! You can disapprove all you want, but I need to know you can keep this quiet! If Leon finds out, or my dad... I don't even want to think about what they'll do!"

Charlene's face seethed with rage as she looked back and forth between Jeremy and me but at least she didn't try to attack him again. She clenched her teeth and her nostrils flared, but she finally said, "Fine. For you, Evie. I will keep quiet. I'll let you have your forbidden flight of fancy. But as soon as this cretin steps over the line, and he will, his ass is mine!"

With that, she turned around, shifted into her four-legged form, and dashed off into the darkness.

I turned to Jeremy, who looked every bit as unsettled as I felt. "You trust her?" he asked me.

"There's no one I trust more," I said. "It's not the first time I've told her something I'd rather die than let my father find out about. But this… I've never seen her react to something I did like that."

Jeremy looked past me, into the forest. "Maybe… maybe you'd better go after her."

I frowned, but I nodded. I stepped up to him, placing my hands on his chest and leaning up to kiss him. "I'll see you again," I said. "I promise. Whatever she does, I'll see you again." Then I reluctantly pulled away, continuing to touch his hand for as long as I could before I shifted to my four-legged form and ran off to return to the village.

As I dashed through the foliage, I couldn't shake a terrible feeling that something was going to make me break my promise to him.

*

I hurried home as quickly as my paws could carry me. When I returned to the village, I caught Charlene's scent trail, and found it led back to her own house. I took that to be a good sign; she had not immediately run to Leon, or my dad. With that worry assuaged, I returned home and showered, washing off Jeremy's scent like I did before. I went to bed, trying to sleep a bit less fitfully this time. I'd gotten away with not smelling like my forbidden lover so far, so I was less worried about that. Now that somebody knew, I was in a lot more danger of being found out.

It wasn't that I did not trust Charlene. To an extent, at least. I knew she would never do anything to hurt me.

However, if she thought Jeremy was a threat, which she very well might, she'd rat him out in a heartbeat.

I woke up the next morning and went through my day as normally as any other; at least as far as anyone who saw me was concerned. I greeted my parents, ate my breakfast, mingled with the pack, and generally did everything anyone expected me to do.

Whenever I saw Charlene somewhere, I kept a watchful, wary eye on her, the hairs on my neck standing on end as I waited to see if she was about to do or say anything that might get me in trouble.

But she acted as normally as any other day, just like I did. Occasionally, she would notice me looking, and I kept expecting her to scowl at me, or something like that. She would just smile and wave, and at one point she even spoke to me. Barely. She walked by me while saying, "Morning, Evie," without stopping.

At least it didn't appear that I was in immediate danger of being ratted on. By around midday, I began to make myself believe that I was in the clear, and that nothing was going to go wrong.

And if I said it aloud I would have jinxed the ever-living hell out of it.

Some time in the early afternoon, we all heard a howl come from the forest, which I recognized as coming from Marla. At once, everyone started buzzing around; that particular howl was one any wolf would recognize as a call for help. Several members of the pack, including Leon, stripped off their clothes and shifted into their four-legged forms, dashing off into the woods to respond.

Less than an hour later, we saw our rescue party returning with the injured Marla, Rudy, Corey and Jana, who came limping along with their helpers supporting them, if not being outright carried. Leon came bringing up the rear, looking all manner of righteously furious as he retrieved his pants.

In spite of myself, I was among those who came crowding around him, trying to find out what had happened. "They were ambushed," he spat. "The Morgandorfs were lying in wait when our hunting party came on them. An unprovoked attack." He ground his teeth together and said, "Well, they're going to learn the penalty for fucking with us!"

He stepped forward once he got his shirt on, and called out to the whole pack. "Everyone!" he shouted. "We've just been violated! The Morgandorfs are pushing us, so it is time we pushed back! Tonight we are going to repay them for this attack! We will get a raiding party together; and slip into their territory under the cover of night and hit them hard where they live! We're going to teach them what it means to draw blood from the Caldours!"

Most of the pack raised their fists and howled along with his bloodlust. I had enough of standing by and doing nothing. I stepped up to him. "Leon, wait a minute!" I said. "What will this accomplish? An eye for an eye, a tooth for a tooth? Is that really going to make things better?"

"We are not going to back down in the face of this kind of hostility!" Leon declared. "We're going to meet it like wolves!"

"But just charging into their territory and attacking them? Do you think they are going to just roll over after that? All that will do is make them even madder! They'll hit us back, and then there will be even more blood! On both sides!"

"What would you have us do?" Terry demanded of me. "Just ignore them? Let them get away with this? Didn't you see Rudy's leg just now? He might actually lose it!"

"But we're talking war here!" I said. "They hit us, we hit them harder, they hit us harder… where does it end?"

"When every damn one of those filthy fleabag Morgandorf scum-suckers is belly up, that's when!" old Tobias spat, practically frothing at the mouth. Several others around him roared in agreement.

I looked around me, suddenly feeling helpless. I could see now there was no stopping this; not when everyone around me was so full of bile and rage.

Then things got worse.

Leon put a hand on my shoulder and looked me in the eyes. "I'm leading this attack tonight," he said. "And as my future bride, I'm expecting you to be there."

I felt the blood drain from my face as he said that. "What?"

"You heard me," he said. "It's obvious you don't have a taste for what needs to be done. But if you're going to lead this pack with me, you're going to have to learn."

He turned back to the rest of the pack as I stood there, agape. "The raiding party sets out at ten o'clock tonight," he announced. "Who's going with me?"

"I am!" a dozen of my packmates shouted at once, raising their hands in the air.

After that, everyone started filing away, most of them looking to go tend to our wounded. I simply stood there frozen, unable to move. What could I do now? There had to be some way out of this… was there a way I could warn Jeremy? How could I? He wouldn't be expecting me, so it was doubtful he would be in our usual meeting place, and I couldn't very well just waltz into Morgandorf territory; his pack would rip me to pieces. Maybe if I came in carrying a white flag or something… it would be crude, but I had to do something…

"Don't do it."

I had been so caught up in my panic and uncertainty I hadn't even noticed Charlene's approach until she spoke. I almost jumped when I noticed her standing beside me, speaking just above a whisper to let no one else hear.

"What?" I said.

"Whatever you're thinking of doing," she said, "don't do it."

"You don't know what I'm thinking."

"Don't I?" she said, and took hold of my arm and started guiding me away, out of earshot of anyone else. "Tell me you're not planning to run off and warn that boyfriend of yours about this?"

"I… no, I…"

"Don't lie to me!" she barked as quietly as she could.

I set my jaw and met her gaze. "Charlene, do you really want this to turn into a war?"

"Evie, wake up! This already is a war! It has been for years!"

"But what are we even fighting over? Land? Game? Something someone said thirty years ago? What is the point of all this? It doesn't gain us anything except more bloodshed!"

"You can argue philosophy all you want," she said. "But this is reality. The Morgandorfs aren't going to back off and stop attacking us just because you're banging one of them!"

"So that's it?" I shrugged pointedly at her. "We just accept it, and keep fighting? There's no way around it?"

"It's called pride, Evie," she said. "And if that's not enough, try survival."

"You know, call me crazy," I said, "but the idea of more fighting and bloodshed seems counter intuitive to that."

"So, instead you want to go out there, warn the Morgandorfs that we're coming, and give them an advantage? If you go out there, you will be betraying your own pack! Is that what you want?"

"What I want is for all this violence to stop!"

Charlene frowned, and stepped back from me. "Okay. If you're not going to let go of your fantasy, even if it means turning your back on all of us, then I wash my hands of you, Evelyn. I am going to be there tonight, next to Leon and the rest of our pack, ripping the Morgandorfs a new one like they all deserve. If I see that dirtball you call a boyfriend, I'm gonna rip out his intestines and use them to make a scarf! And if you get in my way…"

She paused.

"If I get in your way, what?" I asked, nervous.

She hesitated. "You've always been my friend, Evelyn. So don't make me do something we'll both regret by getting in my way."

With that, she walked away, as I stared after her in disbelief. Did she really just threaten me? She was supposed to be my best friend!

I looked around at the members of my pack around me, all riled up and hungry for blood, with me seeming to be the only one thinking differently. Apparently, that made me a traitor to them.

As far as I could tell, my pack was betraying me. This pack, which had always been my whole world, now seemed alien to me.

The only one who understood me belonged to a whole different pack.

As I stood there, I honestly started to wonder if betraying my pack would be such a bad thing right now. It actually crossed my mind. What did I really owe them anymore if this was how they responded to me when I dared to say that maybe they were wrong? What was there really to stop me from just saying, "Fuck you all!" and running off and leaving them?

No. I could not do that. They meant more to me than that. At least I thought they did.

*

The pack assembled near the edge of the woods at ten, just as Leon instructed. Everyone was pumped and raring to go, several of them cracking their knuckles or hooting with excitement, or whatever got their blood pumping harder.

I was the last to join them, and everyone seemed relieved when they saw me approaching. "Finally," Leon said, shedding his jacket. "I want you by my side for this, Evelyn. When the Morgandorfs go to sleep, yours and mine will be the faces of the Caldours that haunt their nightmares!"

I had spent most of the day since the afternoon dreading and anticipating this action. I had paced around anxiously, racking my brain for ways to get out of this. I had considered going back and pleading with him not to do this, but I knew even as the thought formed in my head that it would never work. I had considered running away and never coming back—because if I did run away, I might just have to also do that second part. I had considered going to the Morgandorfs, damn the consequences, and giving Jeremy the heads up to get out of there as fast as his four paws could run.

Ultimately, I'd come to a decision. Ever since I made that call, I'd thought that actually doing it would be the most difficult thing in the world. But as I stood there now, looking at Leon's smug face, so sure of himself, so convinced that he had me where he wanted me, it suddenly became a lot easier.

I marched right up to Leon and said something to him that I'd never said to him before.

"No."

All eyes suddenly whirled on me. Leon's in particular stared at me, open wide. "What did you say?" he demanded.

"You heard me, Leon," I said. "I said no. I'm not going with you."

Dad stepped up beside me. "Evelyn, don't cross me now! Obey your alpha!"

"I won't be party to this!" I declared. "I'm not going to run with you, and I'm not going to fight!"

"Evie…" Charlene said, cautioning me against anything further.

Leon stepped toward me, pointing a finger at me, as he looked me in the eye. "Now listen, Evelyn," he said, "you're going to be my bride, so…"

"No, I'm not."

Yes. I said it.

Everyone around me gasped in shock. Leon recoiled back, his eyes flaring. "*What?*" he spat.

"I'm not going to marry you, Leon," I came out and said. "Because I don't love you. You can't make me just because you are the alpha. I'm not some property that you can just decide what I am going to do."

I was going to say more, but that was when Dad grabbed me by my collar and started pulling me away. "It seems I need to teach her a lesson or two," Dad said apologetically to Leon. "Go on without me. I'll make sure to get her straightened out."

Leon frowned, but turned with a sigh and resumed stripping. "Let's go, everyone," he said, as the rest of the pack started shifting into their four-legged shapes and disappearing into the woods.

Dad pulled me along, making me walk backwards toward one of the houses, where he finally pressed me up against a wall and looked angrily into my face. "What the hell were you thinking there?"

"I think I said pretty clearly what I was thinking," I said. "I don't want to fight the Morgandorfs, and I don't want to marry Leon."

"I meant, what were you thinking trying to defy him? Leon is your alpha! He deserves your respect!"

That's what Dad had always told me. I didn't think I really believed it anymore.

"Why?"

Dad blinked and pulled his head back, as if he could not believe what he'd just heard. "Excuse me?"

"Why should I respect someone who doesn't respect me? He treats me as if I'm a new suit he's picked out to wear to the ball! And you want me to just go along with it because he's the alpha and that's how it is!"

A part of me knew I was getting in way, way over my head, but something would not let me stop at that point. "In fact... is that really so different from how you think of me?"

Dad's nostrils flared, and he pointed a finger at me, inches from my nose. "You take that back right now!" he demanded.

"No, I won't!" I barked, swatting his hand aside. "I've bowed to you and rolled over on command all my life, but now you're going to listen to me! This whole marriage arrangement was never about me! If it was, you would have at least considered asking how I felt about it, instead of just telling me to 'learn to accept it!' All you have cared about is having your daughter married to the alpha, so that you can have your precious legacy on the alpha line! I'm not going to be your fucking bargaining chip!"

"Don't you dare talk to me that way—"

"I'll talk to you however I damn well please for once in my life! I am my own she-wolf, and this is my decision to make! It is my goddamn life, not yours! Or Leon's!"

Dad spent a long while silently regarding me. He huffed and puffed quietly through his nose, while I waited, wondering what he was going to do.

He backhanded me hard across the face. I dropped to the ground, holding my bloody lip, staring up at my angry dad. "I have tried to teach you respect and obedience," he fumed. "I've obviously failed. Now you're going to go back to the house, and you're going to wait for me, while I decide what to do with you."

Then he actually turned his back on me.

Wow. He really did not get it.

I sprang to my feet and ripped my clothes off, and I rushed toward the woods, changing to four legs in mid-stride. I heard my dad shouting, "Dammit, Evelyn, come back here!" before he started to chase after me.

I didn't slow down for a second, regardless of what form of tree or rock or foliage sprang up in front of me. I ran like a beast possessed, dashing and weaving through the forest, hell bent on reaching my destination.

I wasn't sure how closely Dad was following behind, or if he even was anymore. I no longer cared. All I could think about was Jeremy. I could only imagine the chaos about to unfold where he was… and if Leon or someone else in my pack got to him before I did…

It was too much to imagine. I had to get to him first.

I didn't exactly know the way to the Morgandorf village, but my pack had left a scent trail as conspicuous as a neon sign. All I had to do was follow them… knowing they would already be there when I arrived, and praying Jeremy wasn't one of the first ones they found.

CHAPTER FOUR

I could hear and smell the carnage long before I saw

it.

Several minutes before reaching my destination, I heard the howl of a Morgandorf wolf sounding an alarm to his or her pack. I didn't think I could have possibly run faster than I already was, but once I heard that howl, that was precisely what I started doing. I emerged from the forest into what had to be the Morgandorf village to find a hideous scene of chaos and bloodshed before me. Dozens of wolves I knew from my own pack were viciously biting and clawing at dozens of wolves I did not recognize, with fur and blood flying everywhere.

I raised my head and sniffed at the air, trying to locate Jeremy's scent, but with so many wolves running, charging, and jumping about, it was like trying to find Waldo. So I went running towards the fray, hoping I might find him somewhere in there.

I quickly realized my mistake when a random Morgandorf wolf came charging at me, seeing me as just another attacking Caldour. I tried jumping away, trying to avoid a confrontation, but my attacker would have none of that. He continued rushing at me, spittle flying from his bared fangs and his eyes burning with crimson rage.

Unable to escape, I reared back on my hind legs to meet his charge. I tried to be as non-aggressive as I could, trying to only push his attacks away by swatting his claws aside and nudging him back with my head, while ducking away when he tried to bite me. Apparently, he was too caught up in the bloodlust to understand that I meant him no harm. I started to realize I was not going to get away from him without fighting back.

I figured that out a few seconds too late to stop him from finally getting a good bite of me. I yowled with the sharp pain as his teeth sank into the flesh of my shoulder. Many of my pack were used to this kind of pain, from all the fights they participated in for fun. I was the lightweight with no scars, who shied away from inflicting or receiving battle wounds. When his fangs dug into me, it was as if my brain suddenly didn't know how to deal with this kind of pain.

Which I guess was why I wasn't sure what was happening at first, when my attacker was suddenly gone the next instant.

I blinked through the pain in my shoulder and looked up, seeing that another wolf had rushed in and was fighting my attacker off. My first instinct was to think that one of my pack had come to my rescue, but as I looked harder and caught his scent, I realized otherwise.

It was Jeremy.

Jeremy was fighting off his own packmate for me.

The attacking wolf backed off after Jeremy got a good bite into his side, and then Jeremy turned to me. I nodded my head toward the woods, which he understood. As I started running away from the fray, he ran after me.

The sounds of growling and biting faded into the background behind us as we dashed into the trees. I thought we were about to make a clean getaway, when suddenly another lupine shape appeared right in front of us, her fangs bared and dripping as she growled.

This one I recognized immediately.

Despite her ferocious visage, I felt safe enough with Charlene to risk shifting to my two-legged shape in front of her. I rose to my feet and looked down at her. She waited a few seconds before she did likewise, and then I heard Jeremy taking his two-legged form behind me.

"Get out of my way, Evie," Charlene warned.

"Not gonna happen, Charlene."

"He's a Morgandorf, Evie! He's the enemy!"

"Not to me."

She tilted her head, looking at me like a stranger. "So that's it then? You're really turning your back on your own pack?"

"If this is how my own pack rewards me for following my own heart, maybe that's what I have to do."

Charlene growled, her teeth growing longer and pointier, and her eyes turning yellow. "I don't want to hurt you, Evie," she warned, her voice rumbling with an underlying lupine growl.

"You're gonna have to if you want to get to Jeremy," I firmly stated.

She continued glaring at me with those fiery yellow eyes, and I started to think she really was going to attack me. Seconds ticked by as I waited, wondering what she was going to do.

After several long, breathless minutes, she seemed to relax, her eyes turning back to their human brown and her teeth shrunk down to human size. She looked at me with a defeated frown, and said. "Get out of here."

"Just like that?" I said.

"Just go before I change my mind!"

I spared a glance back at Jeremy, before we started moving off into the woods past her. Just as I began to pass Charlene, she suddenly reached out and grabbed my arm to stop me, and turned her head to look me in the eye. "Evelyn," she said. This already could not be good, if she was not abbreviating my name. "I want you to know this makes you a traitor. If I ever see him again... hell, if I see *you* again... well, you better hope I don't!"

She disappeared into the brush after that, while I stood there, too stunned to move. To hear my best friend say those things to me...

Suddenly, my shoulder did not hurt so badly anymore.

Jeremy came up behind me and began stroking my arm. "Are you okay?" he said.

"I don't think I am," I said honestly.

He pulled me into his embrace from behind. "Come on," he said. "We'd better go."

*

We ran for hours through the woods, only stopping when my shoulder started to hurt too much for my front leg to continue supporting it. At that point, I collapsed forward and resumed my two-legged form. Jeremy stopped, and retook his own human shape, kneeling down over me. He took a good look at my wound, and then stood up. "Stay there," he said, "I'm gonna find something to treat that."

"Out here in the middle of the woods?" I said,

 Jeremy was already hurrying off into the foliage, digging around in the bushes, for what, I couldn't imagine.

He soon disappeared from my sight, though I could still hear him rummaging around. As I lay there, pressing a hand to my wound, I started listening to the sounds of the forest around me. I heard the chirping of crickets, the hooting of owls, and the scurrying of small animals in the brush. All of it sounded much bigger than it ever had before.

Being a wolf meant I was more than accustomed to running around without my clothes on, just like I was right then. I couldn't remember ever feeling quite so naked.

Because I'd always had my pack behind me.

What did I have now? I defied my alpha, stood up to my father, ran away with a member of a rival pack and been called a traitor.

I'd been torn over what to do before, when I was expected to marry Leon. Now I felt truly lost. More than ever, I had no idea what to do next.

Jeremy returned with a few bits of plants in his hands, and knelt over me again. "Let me see it," he said. I reluctantly removed my hand from the bite on my shoulder, while he started picking some little flowers from his hand. "This might sting a little," he cautioned. I hissed in pain as he pressed the plants to my wounds, but he kept a hand held tight over me to hold me steady. Then he took a large leaf and wrapped it over my shoulder, pressing it down to hold it in place. "This ought to help the pain, and keep it from getting infected."

I clenched my teeth for a few seconds more, but then the pain started to dull. I sighed as my muscles started to relax, and my hand came on top of his, partly to help hold the leaf in place, partly for… other reasons.

"Where'd you learn that?"

"My pack puts a lot of value on learning herbal medicines," he said. "You never know when you might need to treat something when you're miles from a first aid kit."

"Case in point," I said.

Jeremy lay down on the ground and curled up with me. "You know we can't stay here long," he said. "If they come looking for us, they'll find us. They only have to follow our scent trail."

"And what happens if they do find us?" I wondered aloud. I was not expecting him to know the answer; I just needed to ask it, because I really wanted to know.

"Who can say?" he said. "I guess it depends on which pack finds us first. They'll probably try to kill one of us and take the other one back."

Great. Really comforting.

"Well," I sighed, "maybe they're still too busy fighting each other to worry about us right now. How many of them even know we're gone yet?"

"Glad to see you finding the glass half full," he said.

"Actually I'm coming up with an excuse to just lie here for a while."

Jeremy chuckled. "I can appreciate that."

He wrapped an arm around my back and pulled me against his chest, which I pressed my head against, using him as my pillow.

I think we dozed off like that for a few hours. The next thing I remember was being awoken by the sound of a howl in the distance. It didn't take me long to recognize the howl either.

"That's my alpha," I said in a harried whisper as Jeremy and I lifted our heads. "He's looking for me."

"How's your shoulder?" he asked.

I looked down at it, pulling the leaf away. The area around it was pretty purple and yucky, but the bite wound had closed. "I think I'm okay. Going to leave a scar, though. Guess I'm due for one."

"Come on," he said, rising to his feet and extending a hand down to help me to mine. "We should get going."

"But where can we go where he won't find us?"

Jeremy looked around, thinking. "There's a river about half a mile that way," he said, pointing off into the distance. "He won't be able to follow our scent trail if we cross it."

I nodded, and we shifted to our four-legged forms and ran off in that direction.

Judging by the look of the night sky, it was nearing 4 a.m. by the time we reached the river. I'd never been much of a swimmer, but when faced with the choice of that or whatever Leon might do if he caught up with us, I wasted no time in jumping right in after Jeremy.

The water was freezing, and rushing like mad. My paws worked hard to keep me moving forward, fighting against the tow that worked relentlessly to pull me downriver, away from my goal on the other side. I saw Jeremy reach the shore and climb out, shake himself dry, and then turn his head back to me. I surged forward with a renewed dedication to reach him—

—when something, I'm not sure what, maybe it was a limb or something, but something in the river collided with me, knocking me off my course.

All sense I had of up or down vanished as the current carried me helplessly tumbling along. I could hardly tell if I was paddling at water or empty air. All I could see were indistinct blurs of white water foam and occasional glimpses of the sky. The only time I could tell what was above or below me was the brief time when I went over a few feet of waterfall.

Yeah, that was scary.

Just when I was starting to think I would drown before Leon ever caught up with me, I felt a pair of jaws close around the back of my neck and start pulling me in another direction. All at once, I could breathe again, and I felt dry land beneath my side. I coughed water out of my lungs and shakily pushed myself up on my front paws.

I blinked a few times to see Jeremy shifting to his two-legged form and kneeling in front of me. "Are you okay?"

I shook the water out of my sopping wet fur, making Jeremy recoil and shield himself, before I retook my two-legged shape. "Peachy," I croaked.

"Well, as unpleasant as that was," Jeremy said, "It probably worked out for the best. We're way downriver now from where our scent trail ends, so it'll be that much harder for anyone to find us."

"Great," I grunted as I pushed myself up to my feet. "Next time, let's pack a raft."

Jeremy pulled my arm across his shoulders and helped me continue forward for a ways. By the time we'd made it up the hill in front of us, I finally could go no further and told him to let me down. I fell asleep in his arms shortly after that.

*

I awoke the next morning to see the sun rising over the tops of the trees, with nothing but the sound of nature around me, the morning breeze on my naked skin, and Jeremy's body spooned against my back. Despite everything that had happened, I felt like I hadn't slept this well in years.

I rolled around in Jeremy's arms to see his face. The motion started stirring him, and he grunted and blinked awake, smiling as he slowly recognized my face. "Morning," he said.

I propped my head up on my elbow as I studied his face. "I think this is the first time I've seen you in daylight," I said. "Every time we've been together it's been dark."

"You like what you see?" he asked.

I nodded without any hesitation. "I really do."

"Me too," he grinned, looking down over my body, running a hand along my side and over the flare of my hip. My flesh tingled at his touch, making goose bumps break out across my skin.

I leaned forward to kiss him, bringing my hand up to cup his face. The kiss was light and tender at first, and then steadily increased in intensity. We soon parted our lips and allowed our tongues access to each other's mouths, letting them dance together in a graceful and passionate ballet. Before long, I was humming softly into the kiss, feeling like I wanted to devour him whole.

I moaned as he rolled me onto my back, his hand roughly pawing at my tit. I pressed my crotch up against him, feeling his stiff hardness already at attention and available for me to rub my pussy against. My juices started flowing, spreading wetness along the underside of his cock as ran it through my cleft.

He ducked his head down to kiss along my neck and shoulder while I continued grinding my body against him. He brought his lips close to my ear, and I heard him whisper, "I think I could get used to waking up like this."

My first impulse was to wholeheartedly agree. I definitely wanted to wake up like this more often.

Then I had to go and start thinking about the implications.

"I could too," I said. "But what does that mean?"

"Huh?"

"Are we just going to run away and abandon our packs completely?"

Jeremy seemed to balk at the idea. "I can't say that's the most appealing idea in the world. But I'm willing to do it if it means we can be together."

He stopped what I would have said next by kissing me. I wanted to be annoyed with him, but his kiss was too good not to enjoy, and in spite of myself, I started rubbing against him some more.

Eventually, I struggled to break off his kiss, which was not easy, not just in the sense of getting him to stop. I also had to get myself to stop. "Wait... stop... I mean... yeah, I want to be with you too.

Those are our friends and family back there. If we run away, aren't they just going to keep fighting? How many of them will end up killing each other if we do nothing?"

Jeremy frowned. "But what could we do even if we did go back?"

"I don't know," I sighed. "Something. I just hate the way I left things with Charlene, and with my dad. I don't want those to be the last things we said to each other."

"But you can't go back there with me," he said. "And in fact, didn't she even threaten you if you ever came back?"

"Charlene's bark is usually worse than her bite," I said with a little more confidence than I felt. "Usually. I still don't believe she'd actually hurt me."

"But what about your father? Or your alpha?" he said. "If you go back to them…"

"What about your pack?" I said. "Do any of them know about me?"

"No, but… we've discussed this. If I just bring a Caldour in…"

"How will they know I'm a Caldour?"

He did not have an answer to that right away.

I stroked his face a little. "I do want this," I said. "I want you, Jeremy. I want you more than I've ever wanted anything. But I can't just run away and leave everything else I've ever cared about to burn."

Jeremy gritted his teeth. "We just came all this way…"

"To make sure *my* alpha didn't find us," I finished for him. "I wasn't able to convince my pack to change. Maybe we'll have better luck with yours."

"That's a big maybe," he said.

"But I want to take the chance," I said. "And I'd feel better about it if you were with me."

Uncertainty clouded his face. Knowing he needed some persuasion, I reached down between us to grasp his cock, which had started to soften during our conversation, which I began stroking back to its full hardness. "Want me to convince you?" I smirked.

He sighed with a shake of his head. "You're an incorrigible she-wolf," he said. "Okay, I'll think about it."

"You do that," I said. "After you fuck me good and hard."

"Yes ma'am!" he stated, pressing the head of his cock to my opening.

My legs came up alongside him as he pressed into me, and my fingers clutched at his back. "Nnnnnhhh…" I groaned as penetrated deep inside me.

As he began to thrust, and I began to moan with the pleasure he gave me, I prayed that nothing would tear us apart again. What I wanted to do was risky; I knew that. It would have been the easiest thing in the world to just run away with him and forget about the madness we left behind.

I could never live with myself if I did that. Going back and trying to put a stop to this feud may be the biggest mistake I ever made, but I knew I had to try.

That could wait. Right then, I was there in Jeremy's arms, his cock buried inside me, with no one to stop us. I wanted to savor that while I could.

CHAPTER FIVE

The deer thought he was clever. He knew enough to keep ducking back and forth through the trees to try to elude me, and jumped over every possible obstacle that might slow me down. He jumped a high rock, crossed the stream, and even ducked under a giant root that crossed over a gulley.

He led me on a merry chase, that's for sure, and if I'd been hunting alone, he might have lost me.

Just as the deer cleared an embankment a good five or six paces ahead of me, Jeremy sprang out from where he'd been hiding, taking our quarry by its throat and bringing it down to the ground in a single deadly pounce. In an instant, I closed the distance, locking my jaws onto the animal's haunches while Jeremy choked the life out of it.

With the animal down, Jeremy and I proceeded to eat our freshly-killed prey, tearing out chunks of meat in our teeth and munching them in our jaws. I was as much a fan of a well-cooked meal as the next girl, but there's nothing quite like tasting good, raw meat in your mouth, feeling the blood of your kill dripping from your teeth. *There hadn't been enough occasions,* I thought, *when I'd really taken the time to enjoy the pleasures of being a wolf.*

Jeremy and I had spent the last three days this way, living in the woods, hunting for our food. We'd probably spent more time in those three days in our four-legged forms than our two-legged ones, which was something I didn't think I'd ever done before. It was getting to the point now that it actually was starting to feel weird whenever we did change back to our two-legged forms; I was apparently getting a bit too comfortable in my fur.

We really shouldn't have been waiting; we knew that. The longer we stayed out here in the woods, the harder it would be for us to come up with a convincing cover story. The only reason we were hesitating at all was because the prospect of going to meet Jeremy's pack felt a bit too much like going to face a firing squad.

If they found out I was a Caldour…

After we ate our fill, Jeremy and I relaxed together under a tree, next to what was left of our kill. As we basked in our food coma and the closeness of each other, I contemplated our situation. Living like this was nice, yeah. I wasn't going to pretend that the prospect of running away with Jeremy and leaving both our packs behind wasn't still tempting. But I stood by what I'd said before, I couldn't turn my back on the pack that had raised me while they and Jeremy's pack fought and killed each other.

I eventually sat up and began to shift. My fur receded into my flesh, my front legs extended into human arms, and my muzzle shrank into my face. My tail disappeared, allowing me to sit back against the tree. "I think it's about time, Jeremy," I said.

He lifted his head to look up at me, and began shifting to his two-legged form too. "Are you sure you're ready?"

"We've put this off too long already. Our story is gonna start to sound far-fetched if we keep waiting."

Jeremy sighed. "Yeah, I know. I'm just not ecstatic about having to face other people again. I'm getting used to it being just the two of us."

"I know; I'm enjoying this too. We hunt, we eat, we fuck, we sleep under the stars, and that's our day. It'd be nice if we could just pretend the rest of the world didn't exist and live like that forever, but… you know we can't."

Jeremy grimaced, looking up to the sky through the cover of trees. "So when do we do this?"

"It might as well be tonight," I said, with no more enthusiasm for it than he felt. At least I was giving us a few more hours alone.

We tried to enjoy those hours while we could. We relaxed together for a while longer, and then spent some time just running through the woods on four legs. I never felt freer than when I ran, and having Jeremy beside me made it that much better.

But eventually night came, and we knew it was time to face the music.

We cautiously approached the Morgandorf village in our wolf forms. As we neared the lights and the houses, I started hanging back, growing increasingly nervous. I eventually came to a complete stop, making Jeremy stop and look back at me. In fact, I think I even started backing away.

I knew all the propaganda I'd heard leveled against the Morgandorf pack all my life was just that: propaganda. Jeremy was living proof of that. Still, it was hard for me not to associate this place with the stories of the den of scum and malice that had been spun by my pack. The name Morgandorf was not one I had ever heard spoken in a pleasant context.

And after all, the one and only time I'd been here before, someone had taken a bite out of me. The wound in my shoulder was still healing.

I knew those stories were all exaggerated, colored mostly by hate and hostility, and a need to demonize our enemies. But what was a fact was that I still didn't know how they would react to me.

As I slowly started to retreat, Jeremy padded over to me and gently nudged the side of my face with his muzzle. I whined softly at him, not wanting to move further. But he nodded his head in the direction of the village, beckoning me on. Then he continued, while I reluctantly followed.

Several members of his pack were milling about the village, walking around the burning bonfire in the circle when we entered. Several of them looked in Jeremy's direction as he approached, and when they got a good look at him or caught his scent, a lot of their eyes went wide, and they came rushing toward him. "Jeremy?" "Is that you?" "Where have you been?"

Jeremy shifted to his two-legged form as they crowded around him, while I hung back behind a corner. Jeremy tried to calm his pack brothers and sisters surrounding him, holding his hands up and saying, "Please, please, I'll explain it all later. Can somebody get Ricardo out here?"

A couple of them ran off to go fetch the person he mentioned. And about then was when they noticed me. A couple of them sniffed the air, catching my scent, and craned their necks to see me shrinking back shyly around the corner.

"Who is that?" somebody said.

Jeremy extended a hand to beckon me forward, and slowly, fearfully, I approached. As I neared him, I rose up on my hind legs as I started shifting to my two-legged form, and took his hand. I carefully looked around at the faces around me, full of curiosity and wonder, and not a small amount of suspicion.

The few who ran off before started returning, bringing with them a man in his early forties with salt-and-pepper hair and a short, grizzled beard. The other members of the pack stepped aside to make way for him, giving him the respect that could only be commanded by the pack's alpha. His attention zeroed on me as he approached, looking me up and down after he stopped in front of us.

He finally turned his attention to Jeremy and put on a brotherly smile, reaching out to clasp his hand. "We wondered what happened to you," he said, patting Jeremy's shoulder. "We were just about to send search parties out to the Caldour village to find out what they'd done with you."

Jeremy and I shared an uncomfortable look. "Sorry about that," Jeremy said. "The Caldours actually didn't have anything to do with me leaving." Then we exchanged another look, as he remembered the cover story we had agreed to present. "Well, not directly anyway."

The alpha looked to me again. "So who is this now?"

Everyone else in the pack looked at me or at Jeremy, curious to hear the answer to that themselves.

"This is... Elena," Jeremy said, giving them the fake name we'd decided on. I didn't dare want to give them my real name. "She's a stray from up north. I've been seeing her in secret for a while now."

"Why didn't you tell us about her?" someone said.

"She didn't want to be found," he answered. "She wasn't exactly well-treated by her old pack. Her alpha wanted to force her to marry him." We'd agreed our story might be more convincing if we threw a nugget of truth into it. "So she's been avoiding the pack life for a while. She finally decided to come pay us a visit a few nights ago, but... well, her timing was pretty bad. It was the night the Caldours attacked us. As soon as she showed up, she was attacked. So I took her and got her away from here, and we've been living off the land for the last few days until I finally convinced her to come give us another chance. It took quite a bit of convincing, too. She was sure you all would try to kill her again as soon as she set paw in the village."

They all seemed to study me, especially the alpha. I held my breath, waiting to see if they would buy it. My heart crept up into my throat as the alpha leaned in and got a good whiff of my scent. I kept expecting him to snarl at me and say, "She smells like a Caldour!" or something like that.

But finally he leaned back, and a smile spread across his face. "Well then… I think we should prove you right, shouldn't we?" He reached out and put a hand on my shoulder. "Welcome, Elena. My name's Ricardo, I'm the alpha of this pack."

"Hi," I said through a weak smile.

"You want to join our pack?"

I grimaced. "I don't think I'm ready for that. I just want a place to stay for a while. A place with a roof. And a bed. And cooked food."

Ricardo laughed. "Well, we can certainly give you that much." Ricardo turned to one of the she-wolves around us. "Gina, you look like you're about her size. Maybe you can give Elena some clothes."

"Uh, sure," the woman said, uncertainly.

"In the meantime," Ricardo said, "Jeremy, why don't you take her to your room. I think you two could use a shower."

Oh, sweet heaven, yes! A shower sounded like a godsend right about then.

*

I could have stayed in that shower for hours, luxuriating under the hot spray of water, letting days worth of dirt and debris wash away. Of course, I knew Jeremy would only have so much hot water, so there was a limit to how long I could lollygag.

Jeremy and I had started out the shower together, but he'd eventually decided to get out first, while I wanted to enjoy it a little longer. I don't know if I should call that a good thing or not, since without Jeremy there I had only my thoughts to accompany me. And when I started to think, I started thinking hard.

I was taking a shower in the Morgandorf village. I was in supposed enemy territory, under their roof, being treated as a guest. If my own pack could see me now...

What if they did? What if they came looking for me here? What if they found me? What then?

I turned off the shower when the water started to get cold, stepped out, toweled off, and wiped the condensation off the mirror, getting a good look at myself. I wasn't sure what to make of the girl I saw looking back at me. Was that the face of a traitor to her own pack? In my heart, I didn't feel like one, but I knew anyone from my pack would call me that now.

I wrapped a towel around myself and stepped out into the bedroom, to find Jeremy standing by his dresser, wearing a light shirt and a pair of pajama pants. I stopped and stared at him for a moment. He looked up and saw me looking at him, and said, "What?"

"I think this is the first time I've seen you in your clothes," I smirked.

He glanced down at himself. "You like it?"

"I think I miss the sight of your naked tush," I said.

He stepped forward, taking me into his arms. "All you have to do is ask," he said, and kissed me.

I tried to smile back at him, but it didn't really take. I slipped away from him and flopped down on his bed. Yeah, it was really good to feel a bed beneath me again, but that wasn't quite enough to ease my troubled mind. Jeremy sat down beside me and rubbed my back. "Hey, what's wrong?"

"Tell me I'm doing the right thing here?" I pleaded with him. "Do I know what I'm doing?"

"What do you mean?"

"You know what I mean," I said. "I know this was my idea, but now that we're here, I'm just going out of my mind with doubts. This whole thing has the potential to go horribly wrong."

"Only if they find you out," he said. "And I'll make sure they don't. For all they'll ever know, you're just a stray."

"It's not just your pack I'm worried about," I said, looking up at him. "It's also mine. By now they're probably scouring the woods, looking for me. There's every chance they might come here. The idea that the Morgandorfs might have kidnapped me… that's one of the first things my dad might think of. If Leon doesn't think of it first. And if they do come here, and they find me, what will they do to you? What will they do to *me*?"

Jeremy didn't have a swift answer to that. He shifted his jaw uncomfortably, and finally said, "If the Caldours did show up here looking for you, I doubt my pack would let them deep enough into the village to find you. I think we can rest easy for now."

I hoped he was right. I really, really did.

But my ultimate doubt was the thought that we hadn't really thought this all the way through. We'd come back because we knew we couldn't abandon our packs to fight and kill each other. But now that we were here, and I had been given lodging in the Morgandorf village, what were we supposed to do now? How were we going to stop more fighting and killing from happening? There were a few dozen wolves in each of our packs respectively, all driven by the prejudice and hate that they'd been taught for generations. We were only two. How much could we really hope to change?

Jeremy rubbed a hand over my head. "I can tell you've got a lot going on in that head of yours," he said. "Why don't you give your poor head a rest until tomorrow? We've got a roof over our heads, a bed beneath us, and hot water in the shower. Can't we relax and enjoy this? Besides…" he added, leaning in towards my ear, "when was the last time we made love somewhere other than in the dirt?"

Okay, I had to admit, that improved my mood. I turned my head and looked up at him with a smile.

"Well, okay. I just have one more thing I'm wondering."

"And what's that?"

"Why the hell did you bother putting those clothes on in the first place? Did you just want me to rip 'em off?"

His mouth curled up into a smile. "Maybe I thought it could be fun."

I rolled onto my back, bringing my feet up onto the bed, as he peeled the towel away from me. As I became exposed to his eyes, he ducked down and began kissing my neck and collarbone, while I rolled my head back with a soft moan, stroking the back of his head. He kissed along the slope of my breast, while my feet came up, kicking back and forth to work those pajama pants off his legs.

When he rose up on his knees and stripped his shirt away, I sat up to wrap my arm around his torso and began hungrily kissing his chest. He ran his fingers through my hair as my lips suckled at his flesh, and then bent me back down onto the bed where he kissed me deep on the lips. His hands pawed at my breasts, and my back arched up off the bed, my feet squirming about below us.

I brought my hand down to grasp his cock, which by now was standing stiff and ready, while his fingers started petting my wet, puffy pussy lips. I pushed my crotch up against his hand, urging him to rub harder.

He moved lower, taking my tit into his mouth, cradling it in his hand as he suckled at it. I gasped, rolling my head from side to side as his mouth and tongue pleasured my nipple. I cradled his head, writhing beneath his expert tongue.

As he kissed his way further down my body, my legs parted to welcome him between them. And when his mouth reached the junction of my thighs, I lit off like a rocket, screaming to the ceiling and clawing at his hair.

He put my thighs on his shoulders and hooked his arms around them, holding onto them like the handlebars on a rollercoaster. And with the way I was bucking beneath him, he might as well have been on one. But he held on for the ride he was on, just as I rode out what he was doing to me.

Before too much longer, I realized he was about to get me off. Hard. I wasn't ready for that yet. I wanted him to be in me when I came, and I wanted him to know that in no uncertain terms. I sat up and lifted his head up by his hair, pulling him up to kiss me. His lips carried the tangy flavor of my juices on them.

I grasped his shoulders as I lowered back down and he crawled over me, lining his throbbing cock up with my wet, hungry slit. I reached down to take hold of his cock, guiding it into me as he lowered down between my spread legs. I groaned as I felt his mushroom head parting my folds, slowly penetrating into my depths.

I held him inside me once he finally bottomed out. So many times we had done this out in the woods, surrounded by nothing but trees and animals, where any kind of creature could be coming around the pike at any time. And yet I never felt safer than when joined with him like this, buried inside me, his arms engulfing my body as mine did the same to him.

The same still held true now, when we finally had four walls around us, a roof over our heads and a bed beneath us. Ironically, I felt a lot more vulnerable here than I ever did out in the woods. For that reason alone, this was already the best sex we'd had yet. And we'd barely even gotten started.

He started slowly thrusting, looking down at my face as he did. "No one's going to hurt you here," he said softly. "Not from my pack, not from yours. I'll never let them get close enough."

I brought my hands up to cup his face. "I believe you," I said. I pulled him down to kiss me, moaning softly into his mouth as he continued thrusting.

He gradually built up his rhythm, groping at my breast and planting little vampire kisses on my neck when my head rolled to the side. I focused on flexing my vaginal muscles, trying to squeeze him inside of me in time with his in and out motions.

When he ducked his head to take my tit into his mouth, I finally let loose with that orgasm I'd been trying to hold back from earlier. Ever since Jeremy had introduced me to the feeling of coming with him inside me, I could never get enough of it. I loved having his stiff shaft there for my walls to convulse around, much better than I ever felt getting myself off with my pussy so achingly empty.

He paused his fucking motions as I rode out my orgasm, and continued to hold still after I came down from it, pausing to catch my breath for a moment. But as soon as I recovered, he started moving again, moving me along my way to another release.

I took charge, rolling us over to put myself on top and pushing myself up on my arms, my hands resting on his pectorals as I stared down at him, my hips moving back and forth on his lap. His hands gripped my hips, holding my upper body steady as I rode him.

I stared down at him, not wanting to think about the heaviness of our situation. For right now, I wanted there to be nothing but him, me, and his cock filling me up. I let myself become lost in his slate blue eyes, in his hands reaching up to cup my bouncing breasts, and the sensations shooting up through my body from my loins.

I leaned forward, draping my body across his and wrapping my arms around his head, kissing his face while he stroked my back. He started to grunt, beginning to thrust harder up into me, signaling that he was nearing his release. I worked my pussy muscles more, urging him along, until he finally exploded up inside of me. As we stopped moving and took slow, heavy breaths, I continued to hold him by the head, and kept planting kisses on the side of his face, more slowly now, but with no less passion.

I slowly rolled off to the side, letting his softening dick slip out of me, but keeping my arms about him as I rested my head on his chest. "I think I needed that," I said, my fingers lightly stroking his chest.

"You and me both," he said.

"Really?" I replied, lifting my eyes to his face. "You seem pretty okay to me."

"Don't let my calm face fool you," he said. "I've been just as anxious about this whole thing as you are. I know exactly what all your fears are, because I have them too."

I frowned. "So, all your posturing about how you're not going to let anything happen…"

"It's not posturing," he declared without hesitation. "I meant every word. I'm not going to let anyone hurt you, Evelyn. I'm not going to let them hurt either of us. That doesn't mean I'm not still afraid."

"Well," I sighed, "I guess you're just a better actor than I am."

"I hope at least one of us is a convincing actor," he said. "For both our sakes."

*

I woke up the next morning to find Jeremy's bed space next to me empty. I knew he hadn't gone far; I could still smell him in the house, and I could hear someone moving in another room. I got up, put on a robe, stepped out of the bedroom, and found him hard at work in his kitchen, with cluttered dishes all over the place, and smoke starting to rise from the skillet, as he rushed to lift it off the stove and save the eggs he was cooking. He scrambled—no pun intended—to find a spatula and scoop off what was left of his creation onto a plate.

"I take it you're not much of a cook," I observed.

He looked up at me a bit sheepishly. "I'm not used to having company for breakfast," he said. "My usual breakfasts consist of a bowl of cereal, and maybe some Pop-Tarts."

I laughed a little. "Well, I'll still eat your cooking anyway. It's the least I can do."

"'The least you can do?'" he said. "I'm the one making my home yours here. You're not taking pity on me, are you?"

"Any reason I should?"

"Not that I'm aware of," he said, before getting a look on his face and adding, "Unless you know something I don't?"

I laughed some more, and shook my head.

While the eggs ended up being a little overcooked, the rest of breakfast came out more or less okay. "This actually isn't too bad," I told him around a mouthful of bacon.

"Thanks," he said. "I was starting to worry for a minute."

Of course, that only served to remind me that breakfast was the least of our worries. "You realize we're going to have to go out and face the pack after we're done here."

"Yes," he sighed. "You think you're ready for that?"

"We faced them all last night," I said. "That went pretty much okay."

"That was only for a few minutes," he pointed out. "The real test is going to be interacting with them, going through a normal day, acting like one of them. We have to be able to keep up the ruse that you're just a stray from up north for long term. That's what you need to be ready for."

I sat and thought about it for a moment. Then I looked up at Jeremy with a weak grin and said, "Well, if I could act like I was happy about having to marry my alpha back in my own pack, then I'm sure I can play the part of being someone I'm not. Shouldn't be too hard."

I tried to laugh, even fake laugh at my own comment. It wasn't funny.

"You'll have to watch what you say," he said gravely. "If they start to suspect you're a Caldour, even for a second, it's all over."

"No pressure," I muttered.

"I mean it," he said.

"I know you do," I said, getting up from my seat and walking over to hook my wrists about his neck. "Don't think for a second I'm underestimating the situation. But the more we stress about it, the guiltier we'll look."

He sighed. "Yeah, you're right about that."

"I just have to make sure not to say or do anything to raise their suspicions. I don't mention the name Caldour, or name anyone from my pack, and they shouldn't have any reason to suspect me, right?"

"I hope it'll be that simple," he said.

I kissed him, trying to reassure myself as much as him. "Come on," I said. "Let's go face the music."

I started walking toward the door, when he suddenly said, "You're not trying to get away from my cooking, are you?"

I looked back to my unfinished plate of breakfast, and grinned sheepishly. "Okay, maybe I'm a little scatterbrained this morning," I said as I returned to my plate.

"I wonder why," he said.

So we finished our meal, and then, holding hands we stepped out into the village.

CHAPTER SIX

As soon as we emerged, we saw several more of Jeremy's pack going about their business, many of whom stopped and looked up when they saw me. I suddenly had a very strong compulsion to duck and hide behind Jeremy's back. "They're all looking at me, aren't they?" I asked, looking down at the ground.

Jeremy laughed a little. It was a bit of a dry laugh, but it was a laugh. "Nothing suspicious, remember?" he said. "You're just a new face to them. Don't be more than that."

"Well... can I just be a shy new face?"

He shrugged. "I guess there's nothing suspicious about that."

A strawberry blonde she-wolf with her long curls tied back came striding up toward us, her attention definitely on me more than him. "Hi there," she said. "I'm Tara. You're Elena, right?"

It took me a second to recognize my fake name. "Uh, yeah, that's right. Uh, nice to meet you..." I somewhat awkwardly extended my hand, suddenly feeling like I should have done that in the first place. Tara laughed good-naturedly, and accepted my hand.

"So you're the one who broke the heart of half the ladies in this pack," she grinned at me.

That got me feeling a little less timid and a little more curious. I turned and looked at Jeremy with a raised eyebrow. "Is that what I did?"

Jeremy shrugged again. "Well, I didn't want to sound like I was tooting my own horn."

"Really?" Tara said. "You never mentioned your track record with the ladies? About how she-wolves in this pack have been throwing themselves at your feet since you grew big enough to howl?"

"I didn't think she'd find that very endearing," he defended himself.

I looked at Tara with a tilted gaze. "Did you and he ever…?"

"A few times," she admitted. "During howls, mostly. But there have been a lot of others along the way. And… I think some of them are still pretty attached."

I hesitated a moment, before asking, "Should I be worried?"

"Absolutely not," Jeremy said.

"Maybe a little," Tara said.

"Definitely," said a skinny teenage brunette who came walking up to join us.

"Um, hi," I cautiously greeted the new arrival.

"Elena, this is Maggie," Jeremy said.

"And I'm the girl who was gonna get that wolf before you came along," the newcomer sassed me.

Jeremy laughed. "She has a lot of confidence," he pointed out.

"Bigger confidence than her britches," Tara smirked, her arms folded.

"Can you back it up, cutie?" I said, lightly taunting Maggie. "You ever get with him?"

"Not yet," she smirked, looking me in the eye.

I blinked. "You're right. She *is* bold."

"Hey Maggie," Tara said, "why don't you go find your friends? Touch up your makeup a bit. You're going to need to be in top form if you're going to take her on," she finished, pointing to me.

Maggie pursed her lips, and starting walking away, keeping her eyes on me. "You watch your back," she told me, still wearing a slight grin. "This girl doesn't give up without a fight."

As she disappeared into the distance, I turned to Jeremy and asked, "You don't think she's really gonna try something?"

"Nah, she's just an infatuated kid," he brushed her off. "She's more bark than bite."

I spat out a tiny laugh. "Does that include when she's four-legged?" I quipped.

He laughed back a little bit. "Yeah, pretty much."

"Come on," Tara said, "let's introduce you to some of the others."

She and Jeremy started leading me around the village. "That's Astrid and Kevin," Tara said, pointing to a couple who were busy tending to a row of carefully planted crops. "They're the ones who provide most of our homegrown vegetables. There's a few others with green thumbs around here, but none that put out as many tomatoes. And then over there, that's Jason, Samuel and Doug," she said, pointing to a trio of tough guys in muscle shirts sitting around with open beers by a pile of sawed wood. "They're the best carpenters we have around here. I think they're working on building a new garage for Saul's old pickup." She turned to me and added, "The old one finally got too many termites."

We heard the sound of a sputtering engine, and turned to see a rusty blue pickup truck driving in through the trees. "Speak of the devil, there's Saul now. He was just on a trip into town to pick us up some more food and supplies."

Then we came upon a group of kids playing a little game of baseball. It was a simple game with a pretty soft-looking ball and a hand-carved bat, without much protective gear involved, if any. Some of the kids were actually playing in the buff, the better to suddenly shift to four legs and run between the bases (which of course were some big rocks that had been picked up and placed in the more-or-less appropriate places, not always equidistant to each other). They also didn't seem to have any problem with gender equality in this game, since I saw about as many girls playing as boys. I laughed a little as one of them threw off his hat and shifted to his four-legged shape, and ran up and caught a fly ball in his mouth.

"Who are those?" I asked with a smile.

"That's Tony, Anna, Becky, Nicky, Jaime, August, Luke, Ginny, Charles, Kate, Bobby and Candice," Tara rattled off, smiling brightly the whole time. "And that one's Ricardo's son, Stefan," she added, pointing to the twelve-year-old on the pitcher's mound. "Our little pups. Our hope for the future. And I think some of them are cheating," she chuckled.

Seeing them made me miss the pups in my own pack. I missed little Mia and her beautiful paintings, which she always wanted to show off to anyone, whether they wanted to see them or not. I missed little Jackson, always nipping at the heels of his brother Grant, wanting to go out on adventures with him. I missed little Wayne, and his endless stories of misadventures with this animal or that or trips down to the river or whatever was chasing what through the gulley and got caught…

I wanted to sigh with homesick longing. But that was one of the things I couldn't show to my hosts here.

Still, looking around me, I couldn't help but wonder at the idyllic atmosphere that I could see in every direction. The kids were just the prime example of the simple, happy souls that made up this pack. This in no way resembled the filthy, wanton, scum-filled Morgandorf cesspool that everyone in my own pack had always described. When I took it all in, the years of strife and hostility that had existed between our two packs just made no sense to me. Why would anyone wish harm on the wonderful people all around me? What did any of us have to fight about?

"Ah, there you are," someone said. I turned to see Ricardo approaching us, beaming at me with a welcoming smile. "I've been looking for you all morning. Are you enjoying your stay?"

"Yes, it's beautiful here," I said. "Your pack is… very nice."

"Thank you," he said. "It sounds like your fears about pack life have been laid to rest. Is it so different from your old pack?"

"Not really," I shrugged. "Most of my pack was okay… except for not supporting me in trying to get away from my alpha. He was the big problem."

"Well, you have a much better one here," said a forty-something woman with red hair who stepped up beside Ricardo, slipping a hand through his arm. "And you don't have to worry about this one, 'cause he's already taken," she added, looking up at him with a schoolgirl smile.

Ricardo smiled back at her before looking to me again. "Elena, this is my wife, Laura."

"Really curious when I heard Jeremy came back with a stray," she said. "And a pretty one at that." She looked up at Ricardo again and said, "If I didn't already have this one wrapped around my finger, I might almost feel threatened."

"Um… thanks, I think."

I heard some more shouts and cheers from the kids behind us, and turned my head to look back at the game the kids were playing as one of the kids came racing toward home plate before Ricardo's son made a stellar play, snatching the ball out of the air and chucking it hard to the catcher. "Your pup's got a good arm," I offered.

"He does, doesn't he?" Ricardo beamed. "Already flexing his muscles, trying to show he's got what it takes to be alpha someday."

"Is there competition for that job?" I asked.

"He has an older sister," Laura said. "Her name's Andrea, and she's fifteen. She's probably over by the lake right now. There's some sentiment that the next alpha should be whoever she eventually ends up marrying, instead of her little brother taking the role over her. But it's way too early to decide that yet."

I could only hope whoever she eventually ended up marrying was actually someone she wanted. Because I found myself envisioning some strapping hotshot who thought he was God's gift to she-wolves everywhere trying to marry his way into the alpha position.

"I'm honestly really glad you decided to give us another chance," Laura said. "Of all nights to show up, you had the rotten luck of picking the night when those horrible Caldours showed up looking for trouble! It must have been terrifying!"

I fought hard not to flinch at the spiteful mention of my own pack. "Yeah… real terrifying…"

"At least you were lucky enough to find your Romeo in the right pack," Tara said. "You could just as easily have been saddled with those beasts! Then you might actually have had to worry about being snatched up and forced into something."

This was too surreal. I felt like I was in a mirror universe. This was just the way my pack always talked about this one. And yet, the ironic thing was that Tara didn't know how right she was.

"Elena," Ricardo said, "why don't you join us for a howl tonight? We ought to give you a proper welcome."

I nodded. "I'd like that."

"Wonderful! We'll have a special howl for you tonight. In the meantime, feel free to go where you please."

"Thank you."

As Ricardo and Laura walked away, I turned to Jeremy with an uncomfortable look. I couldn't say what I was thinking in front of Tara, but I was pretty sure he could read me. After all those days in the woods spending a lot of our time in our four-legged forms, we'd gotten pretty good at communicating non-verbally.

"Would you like to go meet Andrea?" Tara asked. "I think she'd love to meet you."

"Uh, sure," I shrugged.

"Come on," Tara said, "the lake's this way."

She started to turn to lead me in another direction—and then stopped suddenly, finding someone standing in her path. The man before us was a large, bald guy with broad shoulders and an ornate neck tattoo, standing with his hands in his pockets, looking at me.

"Oh, I'm sorry Lucius," Tara said. "You were so quiet, and you're standing downwind. I didn't even know you were there."

"Yeah," he said in a deep, rumbling voice. "That was kind of intentional. So this is the new girl?"

Tara took a step to the side, allowing him a better look at me. "Yeah, this is her."

"I'm Ev… Elena," I said, still having to remember to not give my real name.

"So I've heard," he said, taking a small step toward me. Impulsively I shrunk back, feeling like he was studying me, and not in a nice way. "So you're supposed to be a runaway? From up north?"

"Yeah, that's right."

"Hmm," he mused, looking at me intently. "Where was that exactly?"

Was I being interrogated?

"Some place I'd rather forget," I answered.

He didn't look satisfied with my evasive non-answer. "You said you dropped by the night the Caldours attacked," he said. "Run into any trouble?"

"A little," I said. "Jeremy got me out of there before it got too bad."

"Well ain't he just a boy scout, then?"

I started growing nervous. This was the first member of this pack I'd encountered who didn't look like he was buying it. But why, in a whole pack full of wolves, was this guy the only one who looked suspicious?

And come to think of it, why was his scent so familiar? I knew him from somewhere... but how was that possible?

"Well, hope you enjoy your stay," he said. "And don't get in too much trouble with the neighbors."

With that he walked away. Tara, Jeremy and I stared after him as he left. "What was that about?" Tara asked.

I looked at Jeremy. "Who is he?"

"Lucius? Just one of our resident tough guys. Leads a lot of our hunting parties, and... attack groups." He turned a look to me, his meaning starting to become clear. "One of the more aggressive in our dealings with... the... neighboring pack."

I started to get the picture. I didn't doubt that some of the scars that Leon had likely came from this Lucius guy.

Was that it? Was that how I'd smelled him before? Had he shown up in our village at some time that I couldn't remember now? I couldn't imagine when; I hadn't been present for most of the confrontations that happened between the Morgandorfs and the Caldours. But I knew his scent from somewhere…

*

Tara brought us down to the lake where we found a small group of teenagers either swimming or lounging about in their birthday suits, with their clothes either casually tossed aside or folded into neat little stacks. A few of them were sitting about in their four-legged forms, too. They all turned their heads to look up at us as we approached, while I raised a hand with an awkward, "Hi."

"There she is," Tara pointed to one girl whose head suddenly breached the surface of the water. The girl began climbing out of the lake, wringing out her chestnut brown hair, before she stopped with her ankles still submerged when she noticed me.

"Hi, I'm Elena," I said. "You're Andrea? Ricardo's daughter?"

"Yeah, that's me," she nodded, carefully bending down to pick up her towel, never taking her eyes off me. "Did you want something?"

"Just to meet you," I shrugged. "I'm getting to know the pack."

The girl looked at me uncomfortably, looking like she was trying to use her towel more to hide than to dry off. "Did my dad send you?"

134

My brow furrowed. "No, why?"

"I don't know… he just has my schedule worked out for me a lot of the time. I thought maybe he'd want you to get to know the girl who's gonna be married to the next alpha or something."

Now why did that sound familiar?

"Your parents told me that wasn't a sure thing yet," I offered. "Doesn't your brother want to be alpha too?"

"He can have it, for all I care."

"Come on, Andie," Tara said. "We're not here to talk about that. Elena just wanted to be friendly. That's okay, isn't it?"

"Sure it is!" one of the girls sitting around said.

"Totally!" chimed in a boy, who rose to his feet and stepped up beside me. "And can I just ask: this thing with Jeremy, is it serious?"

"Hey, hey," Jeremy objected, stepping in between us and gently pushing the boy aside. "Gear down, Tyler. She's not on the market."

Another girl got up and took me by the hand. "You want to come for a swim with us?"

My worried and defensive face brightened into a smile. "Actually, I'd love to!"

"Come on!" that girl chirped, as she and a few others went dashing for the water and dove in.

I turned to Jeremy as I crossed my arms and lifted my shirt up. "Last one in's a dirty skunk!" I cheered. He didn't quite match my enthusiasm as I hurriedly stripped the rest of my clothes off and raced after the excited kids into the lake. He eventually did join me, shaking his head and chuckling softly as he shucked his own clothes and followed me in.

I bobbed my head beneath the surface and swam about, goading Jeremy to chase me, before I came up for air again and saw Andrea still standing at the water's edge. "Come on, Andrea!" I called. "I came down here to meet you! Don't be a spoilsport!"

She seemed to contemplate it for a second, and then sighed, having made up her mind. She dropped her towel and dove back in.

One of the boys came up beside me as my shoulders rose above the surface. "That's a wicked scar, lady," he said. "Must've been some fight you got in."

I turned my head to look at my right shoulder, having almost forgotten about the nasty bite I'd sustained that night when my pack attacked theirs. "Uh, yeah… real bad fight."

"Was it a Caldour?" the boy asked. "'Cause you should see the scars some of them have given our pack!"

"No, stupid, it wasn't a Caldour," said a girl. "She's from up north, remember? She's never met the Caldours."

"Hope she never does," another girl said. "Some of the shit those bastards have pulled… just sick!"

"Seriously," said another boy. "My dad told me about this time when the hunting party brought down a whole bunch of deer, only to have the Caldours show up, give half our hunting party stitches and limps for a month, and steal the entire kill!"

"How 'bout the time they broke into our food stores and stole the kill we'd made the day before," said another, "and then tried to say they had the right to it because we poached it from their territory! Like come on! Like our guys are supposed to give up a chase just because the animal crosses some invisible line? Get real!"

"Those Caldours are all so anal about those damn borders!" one of the first girls complained. "It's like crossing over it is the eighth Deadly Sin! And they keep trying to push it further back so they can hog more land!"

"They killed my grandfather," someone said.

Everyone turned to the boy who'd spoken. "Yeah, I forgot about that," another boy said. "It was like ten years ago, wasn't it?"

"A raid," the vulnerable-looking kid said. "Middle of the night. Unprovoked."

Naturally, by now I was back to being uncomfortably silent. Jeremy swam up to me, putting a comforting hand on my arm below the water's surface, where no one would see it. I cast him a brief glance, trying as hard as I could not to let my discomfort show.

Unfortunately, my discomfort didn't go unnoticed, but it was misinterpreted. "Hey, maybe we should change the subject," one of the girls said. "I think we're scaring Elena."

"Hey, don't worry, lady," the boy named Tyler said, his grin telling me he still wanted to appear macho in front of me. "We got the best fighters and guards you'll ever find in this pack! No way any stinking Caldour is gonna get his jaws on you!"

"I don't think they'd care about her," a girl said. "She's not a Morgandorf, right?"

"You think they'd make that distinction?" said a boy. "They're Caldours. They'd kill anyone."

Wow. This was worse than I thought. I was beginning to get the real sense of just how deep this feud ran. I always knew there was animosity, but I never got the idea that this was really what the Morgandorfs thought about our pack. If Charlene could hear them now…

"Guys, come on!" Andrea finally spoke up. "Elena just got here and we're being all doom and gloom in front of her. Let's stop talking about the Caldours."

Everyone seemed to agree with that. They went back to swimming around and talking about normal teen things, about what they were planning on doing later, or who was hooking up with whom, or whatever. Normal stuff. A few of them started asking me questions about life with my old pack. Was it very different there? Were there any guys in my life before I found Jeremy?

My favorite question was from a skinny blonde girl named Corrine, who asked, "Was everyone in your pack a douche, or just your alpha?"

"Well," I shrugged, "Not everyone was such a douche, but some of them were." I looked pointedly at Andrea as I added, "My dad was too."

It was enough to get Andrea's attention.

"It wasn't just that my alpha wanted to force me to marry him," I said. "My dad wanted it too. 'Cause he wanted his grandkids to be alphas. So he arranged the whole thing for me."

"What a bastard," a girl named Tammy said. "You didn't have any say in it or nothing?"

"Most everyone in the pack thought this was the best thing that could've ever happened to me," I said. "Nobody seemed to get that I didn't want him. Least of all my dad."

I kept watching Andrea as I spoke. I could see that my words were ringing a chord with her.

"Well, fuck him," a boy named Michael said. "You're better off without those guys. This is the pack with the real wolves!"

"Oh, yeah, like you?" a girl named Sandra taunted him.

"Need convincing, baby?" he challenged, before he began swimming after her.

Things quickly devolved to teenage water hijinks from there. I mostly hung to the side and watched the chaos unfold, letting myself be amused by it as much as I could after everything that had just been said. I reminded myself that I couldn't show vulnerability, but nobody minded if I continued holding onto Jeremy. We eventually decided to climb out of the lake and relax in each other's arms on a spare towel.

I soon noticed that Andrea wasn't joining the fun either. She obviously had some things of her own on her mind. Especially since she kept looking at me.

Eventually, after Andrea had toweled off and dressed, she came up to me and said, "Can I get a moment alone with you?"

I spared a glance at Jeremy, who just shrugged. "Okay, sure," I said. I untangled myself from Jeremy and got my clothes on again, before following her toward the trees, where she found a secluded spot amid the woods.

"What's on your mind?" I asked her.

She looked at the ground uncomfortably. "I'm sorry," she said. "I was rude when you got here. The first thing you asked me was if I was Ricardo's daughter, and I thought the only reason someone would want to know that was because he sent you to find me. Like he arranges everything that happens to me."

"Believe me," I said, "the last thing I want to be a part of is anyone making a girl's choices for her. Not after what I went through."

"I get that now," she said. "So I want to say I'm sorry."

"Hey," I said, reaching a hand out to place on her shoulder. "Nothing to apologize for. If I were in your shoes, I probably would've thought the same thing."

She hesitantly raised her eyes to me.

"Don't sweat it," I reassured her. "Just be glad your dad doesn't already have a husband picked out for you like mine did."

"Don't be so sure," Andrea murmured. "If you ask me, I think he's already auditioning guys for the part."

I blinked, and then laughed. And after a moment, she started laughing with me.

"Well, as long as you get final say in the audition, count yourself lucky," I offered.

"I sure hope so," she said.

"But hey, let's not get too stressed about that now," I said. "You're still young. You've got lots of time. Am I right in guessing you're still a virgin, too?"

She scrunched her face uncomfortably. "Yeah, I am. I mean I've participated in a couple howls, but I'm not quite ready for the 'roll in the dirt' part."

"Speaking of howls," I said, "your dad said there's gonna be one tonight. And apparently it's for me. You think you'll be there?"

She met my gaze with the most honest smile I'd seen from her yet. "You know, I think I will!"

"I want us to be friends, Andie. Can I call you Andie?"

"Sure. Should I call you Ellie, then?"

I laughed at the irony of her trying to abbreviate my fake name. "Call me whatever you want, I guess."

Andrea looked toward the other kids still swimming for a moment, her look starting to take a turn for the mischievous. "Well, if you're gonna be my friend," she said, "I know something we can do."

"Oh yeah?"

"That girl over there?" she said, pointing to a raven-haired girl currently doing tumbles in the water. "That's Lauren. There was this boy I was pursuing for a while, and she knew it. Then the last howl happened, and she went and poached him. I caught her doing cowgirl on him right out in the open. Now it's like I'm invisible to him."

"What a bitch!"

"So you know what I'm gonna do?"

"I can't wait," I grinned.

"I was thinking about finding some of the ugliest worms and spiders I can dig up and sneaking

142

them into her underwear drawer. Want to come with me?"

I grinned wide. "Sounds like fun!"

*

Ostensibly, gathering for the howl that night was no different than the ones I knew from my own pack. A bonfire burned, and the pack gathered around the big rock where the alpha stood above them all. But all the faces and scents were unfamiliar. It was a surreal feeling, entering into this very familiar thing surrounded by very unfamiliar people.

Most of the pack parted as Jeremy and I approached, ushering us to the front of the throng. "Let them through, everyone," Ricardo said. "This howl is for her tonight." We reached the front, and I looked up to the top of the rock to see Ricardo and Laura looking down at us. "Welcome, Elena," he said.

I started to wonder if I was ever going to get used to being called that name.

"Everyone!" Ricardo shouted. "As you all know, we have a guest among us tonight. A lost soul, cast aside by those she once called her family. We of the Morgandorf pack have always prided ourselves on our devotion to family, to friends, and to pack. And if those words mean anything to us, we must be ready to offer them to someone who has lost them. Elena, you avoided us for a long time, despite having found someone in Jeremy. I'm here to say you had nothing to fear from us. And with all of us here, she will have nothing to fear from anything else, will she everyone?"

Everyone raised their fists and howled in agreement. I looked around me at all the smiling faces I saw looking at me. I never could have imagined this happening: I was a runaway, a fugitive from my own pack, being welcomed with open arms by the pack I had always been taught to hate and fear. Just so long as they continued to believe I was someone I wasn't.

For the most part, the looks on their faces told me I was in good shape on that front. They all were smiling at me, welcoming this "Elena" they thought I was.

But somewhere amid that crowd, I could swear I felt one set of eyes looking at me with something less favorable. I couldn't quite locate where it was; there were too many faces to sift through. But someone here wasn't reflecting the same kind of enthusiasm as everyone else.

Ricardo went on, "You all know that our village hasn't been the safest place lately. Especially after the recent attack we suffered from the Caldour pack. And we all know that an attack like that could happen again at any time. Which is why it's more important than ever that we stay vigilant, now that this newcomer is among us, who has more reason than most to be afraid of strange packs. The Caldours are ruthless, they are merciless, and they don't take prisoners. We've all seen the kind of fury they have.

"So if we're going to keep Elena safe, we have to show them that our fury is stronger! We have to make them all see, that the Morgandorf pack does not back down to threats! We do not roll over, or tuck tail and run! If the Caldours wish to threaten us, we will meet them head on! We will fight for what is ours! We will stand our ground, and we will beat them back! And any lost souls who are lucky enough to find their way to us, we will make sure that their home here is safe, secure, and one that they can be proud to call theirs!"

The pack around me erupted in howls, as clothes began dropping to the ground. I wanted to be able to join them, but I couldn't quite get into the spirit of things when he had just spent half of that speech bashing my old pack. But with a little bit of nudging from Jeremy, I finally let myself go. Dropping my jacket, I threw my head back and howled to the sky with everyone else.

All around me, various members of the pack finally got naked and started shifting to their four-legged forms, changing their howls to a more eerie, lupine sound that echoed throughout the night. More and more started to shift, one after another, before Jeremy and I, too, finally shifted, getting down on all four paws and joining in the song, as Ricardo led us from up on that rock.

A scent I had become familiar with earlier in the day suddenly came up beside me. I looked to see a young wolf had joined me by my side, whom I was able to identify by scent as Andrea. We'd had quite the bonding experience today; we hadn't actually found many spiders to sneak into Lauren's drawer, but we found plenty of worms, and even a centipede. Getting into her bedroom undetected had been a bit of a challenge, since her mother had been in the house, and if she'd caught our scent the game would've been over. But we managed to pull it off, and a few hours later, we were rewarded with the sound of distant screaming while we relaxed by the rock quarry.

Oh, how long it had been since I'd partaken in teenage revenge hijinks. It was honestly kind of refreshing, in a guilty pleasure kind of way. But the important thing was that I had succeeded in making a friend out of the alpha's daughter. If nothing else, that could potentially go a long way toward making the kind of peace that Jeremy and I were hoping for.

As she trotted up beside me now, we resumed the howl together, right before several wolves around us started scattering off in all directions. Some of them started fighting and wrestling with each other for fun, while others disappeared into the woods. I looked to Jeremy, who got up on all fours to start towards the tree line, but looked back to me, seeing if I was coming along. I was about to, but looked back toward Andrea first. I wanted her to run with us tonight.

Apparently she got the message, and was more than amenable to it. She got up and started after the both of us.

With that, we dashed off into the woods. I'd almost forgotten how great it was to do this surrounded by a pack. After becoming isolated from my own pack, and after it becoming just Jeremy and me in the woods by ourselves, the feeling of running like this while packmates and friends were all around was… uplifting.

Except that these weren't my packmates. It was getting harder to remember that.

Andrea mostly kept pace with Jeremy and me, staying just a step behind us the whole way. We didn't catch the scent of anything we wanted to hunt tonight; we weren't looking for it anyway. We just wanted to run. We just wanted to be wolves together.

I don't know how long we ran for, dashing through the trees, leaping over banks and rocks and gullies. But eventually we tired ourselves out, and collapsed in the middle of a clearing to catch our breath.

We slowly shifted back to our two-legged forms as we lay there panting, and I heard Andrea say, "I think that was the best run I've ever had!"

"Wasn't so bad for me either," I chuckled. "Jeremy?"

"Well, I can think of worse experiences than running with two she-wolves beside me."

I lifted my head, giving him a mock-chiding look. "Don't you be getting any weird ideas, mister!"

He just laughed back.

As we lay there, another wolf came trotting up to us. I lifted my head as he neared, and then he shifted to his two-legged form to look down at us. I found myself looking up at the bald head and hard-chiseled face of Lucius, the one who seemed interested in interrogating me earlier in the day.

"Oh, hey Lucius," Jeremy casually said.

"Getting settled in?" Lucius asked me.

"That's okay, isn't it?" I cautiously asked, getting the suspicion he wasn't as keen as everyone else on me staying here.

"Of course," he said, not sounding like he completely meant it. As he looked me over, his eyes seemed to zero on my shoulder. "How'd you get that scar?"

I looked to my shoulder again. "Bad fight," I said, trying not to remember the fight that happened that night when my pack attacked theirs. "I'd prefer not to talk about it."

"I'm sure you wouldn't," he said.

He seemed to study me for a moment more, while I met his gaze. I started to grow very nervous, convinced that at any moment he was going to say or do something more that I wouldn't like.

"Watch your back," he finally said, before returning to his four-legged form again and trotting away.

We stared after him as he left, before Andrea finally said, "Did you do something to him or something?"

Did I? I didn't think so, but could I be sure? I knew I'd smelled him somewhere before, but where?

And why was he curious about my—

All of a sudden the answer hit me.

And a cold shiver ran down my spine as it did.

Jeremy seemed to sense it, sitting up and reaching out to rub my unscarred shoulder. "Hey, are you okay?"

I couldn't say what I'd realized in front of Andrea. So for now, I just said, "It's nothing. But I think I'm kind of tired. Do you think we could turn in early tonight?"

"What?" Andrea said. "I thought we were having fun?"

"A bit too much, maybe," I said. "Nothing we can't have more of tomorrow, right?"

"But I'm not tired!" Andrea insisted.

"It's okay," I said. "You can do what you want, Andrea. I just want to go back to the room with Jeremy for now."

Andrea looked at me with a furrowed brow. And when I looked at Jeremy, I saw him giving me the same look. "Please?" I asked him.

He finally sighed and shrugged, and said, "Sure, that's fine."

Jeremy and I got to our feet, before I briefly looked back to Andrea and said, "I'll see you tomorrow."

She continued looking perplexed, even as she waved to us. Jeremy and I shifted to our four-legged forms and headed off into the woods, making our way back to the village.

*

Not many of the pack were still in the village when we got back, so no one paid much attention to us as we made our way to Jeremy's house. That was how I wanted it. We returned to our two-legged forms on our way in the door.

Once we were safely inside, I preceded Jeremy into the bedroom, hugging my arms to myself as he came up behind me, rubbing my shoulders. "Hey, Evelyn, talk to me," he said. "What's wrong?"

I turned around and looked him straight in the eye. "I finally figured out why I know Lucius's scent. I know where I've smelled him before."

"Where?"

I hesitated before answering, setting my jaw. And then I pointed to the scar on my shoulder. "He's the one who gave me this."

Jeremy blinked as comprehension dawned on him. "So then…"

"The night of the attack, he was the one who attacked me. And he knows it. He remembers giving this scar to me. He knows I'm a fake!"

"Well… we don't know that for certain," he said. "He just knows you were there that night. Everyone knows that. We told them right to their faces. If he tries to say anything, can't we just say he mistook you for a Caldour and wrongfully attacked you?"

I gritted my teeth, wanting to believe it would be that simple. "But it's not just me," I pointed out. "You were there too that night. You fought him off of me, didn't you? …Come to think of it, why are you only realizing now that was him? Shouldn't you have recognized your own packmate from the beginning?"

"Well, I wasn't really thinking about faces or scents at the time," he said. "The only thing I knew at that particular moment was that someone was attacking you. I didn't have much of a chance to think about who it was."

"You thought about faces and scents enough to recognize mine," I pointed out.

He shrugged. "Yeah. I guess I did. You're just special that way."

Yeah, I won't deny it was real tempting to kiss him after that. I blinked a couple times and started leaning up to his lips. But then I made myself pull away, turning my back to him. "No! Don't try to distract me with sweet talk! This is serious!"

"So am I," he said. "Is that still sweet talk?"

I slowly turned back around to him, and this time I let him take me into his arms. "What if he rats me out?" I whimpered against his chest.

"Even if he suspects you, he can't prove anything," Jeremy said. "Our cover story will still hold. We have to go on believing that."

I let out a heavy breath. "I don't think I've ever felt so paranoid in my life!"

"Evelyn, look at me," he said. I lifted my eyes, which I only realized then were shedding tears. "I am not going to let anyone hurt you. I defended you against Lucius once before. If he tries anything, you better believe I'll do it again. The same goes for anyone else."

I smiled weakly, and pressed my face against his chest again, holding him tightly.

We eventually made our way to the bed, where I crawled atop him and made out with him hard, rubbing my crotch up and down against his hardening dick, while his hands roved all over my back and felt up my butt. My stiff nipples scraped along his pectorals, sending tingles of excitement up through my boobs.

He rolled me onto my side and cradled me in his arms, holding me to him by my neck and hip as he devoured my mouth, while my hand stroked back and forth from his hair to the side of his neck. My legs fidgeted about, my upper leg stroking along the length of his. And all the while his cock kept poking into my lower belly.

I arched my back when he slid down lower, bringing his mouth down to my tit. My arm fell back away from him and my fingers curled up, digging into the sheets, as my head rolled back and I moaned. He started moving his body down, keeping his suckling mouth fastened to my nipple until the point when his body had simply moved too low to maintain contact there.

He slowly worked his way down, kissing his way along my belly, while I squirmed and panted beneath him. Finally he reached the point he was searching for, giving me the best kind of comfort he could with his mouth between my legs. I gasped sharply, my head snapping back and my fingers digging into his scalp. My body made waves under him like a rug being shaken out.

I ultimately came twice with him going down on me like that, before he lifted his head and rolled me onto my side. With that he came up on my back, spooning up behind me, gripping his cock to aim it at my entrance. I lifted my upper leg as he enveloped me from behind, and with little resistance he slipped inside me.

We made love slowly and tenderly at first. He thrust into me gently from behind, wrapped about my back, his hand seemingly never coming away from my breast and his lips seemingly never coming away from my neck. It was exactly what I needed at that moment; in his arms, with him buried inside me, I felt safe, no matter what was happening outside.

I don't know how long we went on like that for. It may well have been more than an hour. As far as I was concerned, it could have gone on forever. The longer it went on, the longer I wanted it to. I wished we would never have to leave that room.

It was made even better by the sweet nothings that Jeremy kept whispering in my ear. "You're safe with me," he would say. "I'll hold onto you forever." My favorite was "I'll never let you go." And then there was even an occasional "You're so beautiful." That made me feel pretty good, too.

After he finally came, we relaxed and caught our breath, not bothering to take him out. We just stayed like that with his softening dick still inside me, luxuriating in each other.

We eventually fell asleep like that, with him still buried in me. I remember waking up the next morning, blinking at the sunlight streaming through the window, and finding him still spooned up behind me. He had finally slipped out of me during the night, but I was still enveloped in his arms, and we were still together in his bed. That was all I needed for the moment.

I turned in his arms just enough to reach a hand behind his head and play with his hair until he grunted and blinked awake. He smiled at me, and without a word to each other, we kissed.

As I rotated around to put my front to him instead of my back, I started voicing the thoughts I'd had last night. "Can't we just stay here?" I said. "I don't want to leave this room. I like it right here, where there's no packs, no feud… no guy named Lucius watching me."

Jeremy chuckled a little. "I know how you feel," he said. "We kind of had that in the woods, didn't we?"

"Don't remind me," I muttered.

"We can stay here for a little longer at least," he whispered.

I grinned, getting his meaning completely. I threw my arm around his neck and kissed him deeply.

I bent and started kissing all over his chest. I moved up and down and forward and backward and side to side, not missing an inch of his flesh. He ran his fingers through my hair, caressing my scalp, and rubbing his other hand over my back. I started to move lower, coming down to his already stiff cock, grasping it in one hand and cradling his balls with the other as my mouth wrapped hungrily around the head.

I made slow, languid bobbing motions with my head, lifting my eyes to watch his expression as I did. I also kept humming softly around the stiff thing filling my mouth. "Mmm... mmm... mmm..." He continued to stroke my hair, and then rolled his head back, grunting in appreciation.

I continued blowing him, enjoying the feel of his cock in my mouth, for as long as my pussy could stand to remain empty,. which that morning was not all that long. Pretty soon my cunt was dripping with anticipation, hungry to feel the thing between my lips parting my other lips again. I sat up, giving his shaft a few more soft strokes, as I climbed atop him, straddling his lap. I aimed him at my opening and lowered down.

I breathed hard as I started to ride him, his hands stroking up and down my hips. My hands felt up his rippling abs as I stared down at his eyes, which looked back at me lovingly. I worked my inner muscles, squeezing my pussy walls around his cock, hugging him inside my most intimate of places.

We spent a good long while with me riding him like that, going a little faster than we had gone the night before, but not by much. We were a bit more energized now, and I felt less in need of comforting than I had, but we still wanted to take our time and enjoy this. So we went slow but hard and deliberate, my hips churning on his lap with steady motions. But while my hip motions were steady and rhythmic, the motions of my head and upper body were more all over the place. When his hands came up to grope my boobs, my head rolled about, moaning loudly. Eventually, I did actually start moving faster, starting to get closer to an orgasm and working to get myself off. Jeremy grabbed my hips again, holding on for the ride as I neared my release, gradually going from slow, deliberate motions to starting to ride him like a bucking bronco.

When I came, my back arched and my head threw back, releasing a loud shriek of ecstasy. I was barely aware of his seed erupting up inside me as I became lost in the moment of my orgasm.

After I came down from my climax, I lay flat atop Jeremy's chest, tenderly kissing and nibbling his neck. He softly stroked my back, moving his fingers up and down my spine, getting low, happy coos out of me.

"As much as I'd like to do otherwise," he said, "we do have to step outside eventually."

"Do we have to think about that now?" I whimpered. "I'm in a good mood."

"We don't have to do it now," he said. "Just eventually."

"'Eventually' can take its sweet time for all I care," I said. "Right now I want to keep you here until I drain you of all your fluids!"

Jeremy groaned as if exasperated, but smiled while doing it. "Work, work, work," he grinned, and kissed me.

<u>CHAPTER SEVEN</u>

We spent a couple weeks living like that, living among Jeremy's pack, pretending I was someone I wasn't. And for the most part, no one seemed to be the wiser. Most of the pack welcomed me as one of their own; as far as anyone was concerned, I may as well have been a Morgandorf now. I wasn't quite sure how I felt about that. It made me wonder if I would ever be welcomed back among my own.

For that matter, why did I have to carry any kind of a label at all? Why did I have to identify as Caldour or Morgandorf or anything like that? If I were completely honest with myself, this wayward Elena with no pack affiliation anymore felt more like me than my true identity. Who was Evelyn Godfrey of the Caldour pack anyway? That name felt like the name of a stranger.

So it took hardly any effort on my part at all to embrace my ruse. Especially when I had the likes of Tara and Andrea to make me feel right at home using it. My days would be spent wandering the village with Tara, getting to know the ins and outs of the place, swimming in the lake with Andrea and her friends, gathering herbs or hunting in the woods, exploring the surrounding forest, trading stories (slightly edited for content), and just generally being friends together, as much as I had with anyone from my own pack.

Andrea in particular became interested in learning more about my life with my old pack. As long as I didn't mention any names, at least no real ones, I felt like I could be as honest as I wanted to be. I told her all about how my parents raised me, particularly about how controlling my dad was, since that seemed to be what interested her the most. She also wanted to know about things like my first time with a guy, how old I was, and what it was like, and all that. While she admitted she still didn't think she was ready to try it for herself yet, she was still fascinated with the idea of it, and I could tell she was thinking long and hard about when she would be ready to let it happen for her.

I ran with Jeremy's pack, I hunted and howled with them, I ate with them, sang with them, and traded stories and jokes with them. Even if I wasn't a Morgandorf in name, I felt like I had a pack again.

And unlike before, no there were no expectations put on me. Everyone accepted that I was with the guy I wanted already, and no one was trying to pressure me to marry someone else. I didn't have my dad expecting me to fulfill his ambitions for him, or a slick alpha claiming me as his. If anything, the alpha here seemed like a better father figure than my own dad.

The only thing that did anything to crack my happy illusion was the ever-looming presence of Lucius hovering about, always watching me. So far, nothing had happened; he obviously hadn't mentioned anything to Ricardo or anyone else. Maybe because he couldn't prove anything. He knew I'd shown up that night, and he knew he attacked me and that Jeremy fought him off, but that didn't necessarily follow that I was a Caldour.

But I could tell he was suspicious; it was all over his face whenever I saw him. And whenever I did see him, his eyes were always on me, carefully watching my moves. I would be huddled over some little project that Andrea and her friends were guiding me in, and I would get a cold shiver down my spine, and lift my head to see his hard-lined face watching me from across the way. I would be going for a dip in the lake, and when my head came up above the surface, there he would be back atop the hill, paying attention to nothing but me. I would be on a hunt with some others, chasing down a deer and catching its neck in my jaws, and as we all started to feast on the kill I would catch his scent, and find him lurking about among the trees. Any time I felt like I was enjoying a pleasant day, just doing simple things with good company, sooner or later he would always be there, casting his shadow over me.

I kept wondering, why didn't he just make a move already? If he suspected I was a Caldour, why wasn't he trying to prove it?

Maybe he was just trying to stalk me until the psychological pressure got me to crack. I wasn't completely prepared to say it wouldn't work, either.

I confided in Jeremy one night while we were curled up in his bed, his arms around my naked body, his fingers lazily strumming my hair while my head nestled in the crook of his neck. "I don't think I can take much more of Lucius lurking around spying on me," I said. "Part of me wishes he would just rat me out and get it over with."

"You know he's not going to do that as long as he can't prove anything," Jeremy tried to reassure me.

"I know," I grimaced. "I have a terrible feeling he's gonna do something much worse."

"Something worse?" he said. "Like what?"

Frowning, I brought a hand up to my shoulder, which still sported the evidence of what Lucius had already done to me. "He's already scarred me once," I said. "Something tells me he doesn't plan to stop there."

"He can plan all he wants," Jeremy said, "but I'll rip his throat out before I let him lay a paw on you."

"You know you can't watch me twenty-four hours a day," I said. And then almost under my breath I added, "Unlike him."

"Hey, don't be so sure of that," he said. "You want to know something about that night of the attack?"

"What?"

"The whole time the attack was happening, it never occurred to me that you might show up. I was just trying to hang back and avoid the fray. But then I got some kind of… spine tingle, I guess you could call it. And then I just sort of knew to move to the edge of the village, and I found you with Lucius's jaws attached to you. I don't know how, but it was like I just knew the moment it happened."

"So what, you're saying you're psychic or something?"

"Maybe when it comes to you and trouble," he said. "I'm betting if Lucius tries anything with you again, I'll know. And then I'll rip him apart."

I rolled my eyes slightly, grinning. "You say the sweetest things to me," I smiled, and then kissed him.

We made love tenderly that night, which made me feel better and safer like it always did. For a time, I was able to feel reassured again.

And then the next day came.

*

For the most part, it was a day like any other. We joined Tara and some others for some breakfast. Maggie came along and started whispering very suggestive things to Jeremy, even going so far as to blow lightly on the back of his neck before I shooed her away. Everyone around us had a bit of a laugh at Jeremy's discomfort. After that, I joined Andrea for a little run and a few more friendly games with her friends. I got lunch with her, and then rejoined Jeremy later in the afternoon. Everything seemed to be fine.

And then, around the early evening, we heard the howl.

Any wolf would recognize it. It was a howl of distress, calling for help. As everyone turned in its direction, about a dozen members of the pack immediately started running for the tree line, stripping their clothes off and shifting to their four-legged forms. Impulsively, I started going with them, and I heard Jeremy following close behind.

We reached a clearing in the middle of the woods, where four wolves were keeping guard around two others currently in their two-legged forms. One of the two was a guy named Russell, who lay on the ground, gasping for breath, while his packmate named Shane knelt over him, pressing his hands over the bloody wound in Russell's neck.

One of the rescue party named Daniel shifted to his two-legged form to ask, "What happened here?"

"It was the damn Caldours!" Shane spat. "Surprise attack! They came out of nowhere! We didn't even smell them coming until they were right on us!"

Another one named Beverly shifted to two legs and hurried to take hold of Russell's ankles. "Someone help me carry him!" she said. "Let's get him back to the village, quick!"

Several more of the party shifted as well, gathering around Russell to lift him up, never letting the pressure off his wound as they carried him back to the village with us.

All of the pack was gathered to greet us when we got back, seeing us carrying Russell with hands stained red covering his neck. "Somebody get Leonard," Shane shouted, calling for the village doctor. They handed him off, carrying Russell away to the infirmary.

Ricardo and Laura were quick on the scene, seeing the blood on the hands of Shane and the others who carried him. "How bad is he?" Ricardo asked.

"I was afraid the Caldours might have taken his whole head off," Shane said, shaking his head. "I could swear they were laughing when they did it, too. More like jackals than wolves," he added, his voice dripping with venom.

"That settles it," someone said. "We were stupid enough not to hit them back when they invaded our village before. Now they do this! How much more do we stand for?"

"We gotta go to them!" someone else shouted. "Show those Caldour bastards who's boss!"

Several of the pack roared in agreement. It was just like before my own pack launched their attack. The whole pack was crying out for blood, and if something wasn't done to stop them, they would get it. The last thing I wanted was to see another full-on battle.

"Now hold on, everyone!" Jeremy called, stepping into the middle of the crowd. "We should be more focused on helping Russell than getting revenge. What's more important to us: our packmate alive, or our neighbors dead?"

"You really want to let them get away with this?" somebody spat.

"Is this attack really any different than the things we've done to them?" Jeremy asked.

I tried to throw in my two cents, stepping up by Jeremy's side. "This isn't what I wanted when I came to this pack," I said. "I wanted to find a safe place to live, and you all promised you'd give me that. Is this how you're going to do it? By dragging me into a war?"

"If we don't do something, none of us will be safe," someone else said. "Those Caldours would kill us all if they could!"

"Is violence the only way to keep us safe?" I asked everyone. "There's got to be other options!"

"You're awfully soft on the Caldours," said a voice. Turning to its source, I found Lucius stepping forward, regarding me suspiciously as always, with the subtle hint of a grin on his face. "Why is that, I wonder?"

I looked back at Lucius, not answering at first. I knew he was baiting me. I didn't want to say anything that I thought might incriminate me.

Fortunately I had Jeremy there to come to my rescue. "Can you blame her for not wanting her new friends, which a lot of you are to her now, to fight and kill, or be killed in a bloody war?"

Tara stepped forward, trying to be as frankly nurturing as she could. "Elena, I wish it was that simple. I wish we could just sit down and talk this out with the Caldours…"

"Well why can't we?" I asked.

"You don't understand," she said. "It's just not that simple."

"Yes it is!" someone interjected. "It's perfectly simple! They're filthy Caldours! They only understand blood! We gotta speak to them in their language!"

Ignoring her less tactful packmate, Tara went on, "There's just too much bad blood between us. This conflict isn't going to go away just by talking it out."

"And who'd want to share breath with those Caldour scum anyway?" said someone else.

"All right, everyone, let's settle down," Ricardo said. "Elena, I get what you're worried about. I wouldn't wish for a war either. But making peace with the Caldours isn't an easy prospect."

"That doesn't mean we have to keep waging war!" I insisted. "Where does it end if we do?"

Ricardo paused, and finally said. "We'll leave it up to Russell. If he lives, we'll hold back from any retaliation. But if he dies, then we make the Caldours pay!"

Several groans went up at that decision. "That's my order!" Ricardo barked. "Jeremy was right about one thing. Our priority right now is making sure our packmate lives, and as long as he still does, that'll stay our priority. No vendettas without my approval! Is that understood?"

The pack generally seemed to accept Ricardo's command, but they didn't look like they were very happy with it. The assembled throng started dispersing, going back to whatever business they had, but several of them were whispering among themselves, and I could tell what they were saying was not nice.

I was relieved at least that Ricardo had stopped them from going for blood immediately, but I knew it was far from a lasting solution. And the fact that it all hinged on Russell pulling through was all the more reason to hope for his recovery. But there had to be something more I could do than just wait and hope.

Jeremy put a hand on my shoulder. "Come on, let's go see him—"

But I was already marching toward Ricardo and Laura, who no longer had anyone standing around them. "Ricardo," I said, "isn't there anything else we can do to end this? I didn't leave my old pack just to see my new one and another one slaughter each other."

Ricardo sighed. "Elena, I wish it were that easy. But I can only lead my pack where they want to go. And if what they all want is to fight, what can I really do to stop them?"

"Maybe there's something *we* can do," Jeremy said. "We all keep telling ourselves there's no hope of peace with the Caldours, but when was the last time anyone tried?"

"I don't think anyone here wants to," Laura said. "There's too much hate to set aside."

"Maybe not as much as you think," Jeremy said. "I can tell you that not everyone hates the Caldours as much as you think. I've never felt any hatred for them."

"And they've definitely got no reason to hate me," I said, though I wondered to myself if that was really true. "What if we tried reaching out to them? Jeremy and me? Wouldn't it be a start?"

Ricardo and Laura looked at each other uncomfortably. "It would be a dangerous start," Laura said. "You can't be sure they won't just kill you on the spot. Especially you, Jeremy. Just for being a Morgandorf."

"It's certainly what a lot of us here would want to do if a Caldour showed up here."

A knot tightened in my stomach. If he only knew...

"That's a chance we're willing to take," Jeremy said. "Even if they do try to attack us, it's worth the chance to avoid them attacking all of us again."

The two of them regarded us for a while. "This is a very risky thing you're suggesting," Ricardo said. "I can't give my blessing for this... but I suppose I can't stop you either."

That was enough for me. Before I knew it, I had jumped forward and thrown my arms around Ricardo's neck. He grunted slightly, and patted my back. "All right, now," he said. "That'll do."

I blinked my eyes open and got back down on my feet, blushing slightly. "Um, sorry."

"Come on, Elena," Jeremy said, taking me by the arm. "If we're going to do this, we ought to get going. We need to decide what we're going to say."

The true meaning of that was not lost on me. We were in fact talking about going back to the pack I had abandoned, with a Morgandorf in tow. And if they asked, I was going to have to tell them I'd spent the last couple weeks among the Morgandorf pack. I could definitely see this going very badly.

Jeremy and I spent the better part of an hour discussing how we were going to approach this, never quite coming up with any one perfect plan that we were completely happy with. It was getting full on dark by the time we finally decided the only thing to do was to go there and just make the best of it.

Once we'd made that decision, I slumped my shoulders with a sigh and accepted it, absently turning my head to look around. And in so doing, I happened to notice a small circle of pack members gather around, whispering conspiratorially amongst each other. I couldn't hear what they were talking about, but by the looks on their faces and the way they kept looking toward the woods in the direction that the Caldour village lay, I got the impression they had trouble on their minds.

And leading the group was Lucius.

"What are they up to?" I wondered aloud.

Jeremy turned his head to look in their direction. "No good, I'd say," he said.

"You think they're planning to go behind Ricardo's back and attack the Caldours anyway?"

"I wouldn't put it past Lucius," he said.

"We should tell Ricardo."

Before we could do anything else, though, the group of them were already starting to head for the tree line. "I think we might not have time for that," Jeremy said. As they disappeared into the woods, Jeremy and I went hurrying after them, knowing that if they got to the Caldour village before we did everything would quickly go to hell in a hand basket.

No sooner had we moved out of sight of the village, than we were each grabbed by two figures appearing from our sides. I was suddenly being held by the arms by one of Lucius's cronies named Brock, while another one named Regan got hold of Jeremy. And then Lucius appeared from around the trees ahead of us, flanked by his followers Riley and Ennis. "Going somewhere, newbie?" he asked, directed mostly at me.

"We could ask you the same thing," Jeremy said. "You're not planning to attack the Caldours, are you?"

"Maybe we are," Lucius said, folding his arms. "You got a problem with that?"

170

"Ricardo does!" I reminded him. "Or did you sleep through the part where he told us all not to do that?"

"Ricardo is a pushover!" Lucius spat. "He would've done the sensible thing and let us get justice for Russell if you hadn't whispered in his ear and told him not to. Which I find interesting."

"Why do you care so much about the Caldours?" Riley probed. "It's almost like you're worried about your own pack."

"But the Caldours aren't your own pack… are they?" Lucius said, looking me in the eye, daring me to admit that they were.

I said nothing, keeping my jaw set.

"Go on," he said. "Keep pretending. Keep your secrets."

And with that he nodded to the two guys holding us, who started pushing us along in another direction. "Brock and Regan are gonna keep you two company while the rest of us pay your precious Caldour pack a little visit they won't soon forget. Enjoy yourselves while we're gone."

"Come on," Brock said, shoving me along.

"Let's go, Caldour-lover!" Regan spat at Jeremy.

"Make sure they don't let anyone know what we're doing," Lucius commanded. "Now or later." And then he and his goons were gone, into the woods to wreak their havoc.

I didn't know where they were taking us, and I had no intention of finding out. I tried opening my mouth to howl for the pack, but I only got a brief hoot out before Brock clapped a hand over my mouth. "None of that, Caldour trash!" he said.

Fortunately, his bringing a hand to my mouth forced him to release my other arm, allowing me to shove an elbow into his gut. He gave out a winded grunt as I started wrestling myself out of his grasp.

But Brock wasn't one to back down. Even as I started wiggling away, he kept fighting to regain a hold on me, grabbing at my wrists and arms while I tried to kick him away. And out of the corner of my eye, I could see that Jeremy was not remaining idle either, fighting against Regan just as fiercely.

We remained in a holding pattern with no one gaining the upper ground, until a small feminine voice said, "What's going on here?"

Everyone looked up to see Andrea standing there, looking at us wide-eyed. But Jeremy and I only remained idle for a moment, before we each jumped our would-be captors, pinning them to the ground. "Andrea, get your father!" I told her. "Lucius is going behind his back! He's gonna attack the Caldours!"

"What?"

"Just go tell him, quick! Jeremy, come on!"

Jeremy and I bolted off, quickly shifting to four legs as we dashed into the foliage. I didn't stop to listen if Brock and Regan were following behind us; I had other things to worry about. A bloodthirsty

Morgandorf was headed for my pack with murder in mind, and I had to stop him.

I had no time to think about what would likely happen when my pack saw me again.

*

We didn't stop running until we reached the edge of the forest, where the trees opened up into my old village. So far, nothing appeared to be wrong. But Lucius's scent was here, clear as day.

I spotted Leon out near the edge of the village, looking across the pack. Lucius only had two helpers backing him up, and with an attack force of only three, it stood to reason that he would be trying to go straight for the jugular by taking out the alpha. Moments later, I located Lucius and his goons, creeping along on four legs downwind of Leon, slowly advancing on him, their tails twitching in impending attack.

Jeremy and I came rushing out of the woods to intercept them. Leon spun and noticed the attack just as Lucius came leaping at him with fangs bared. But he only had time to get Leon down on his back before I barreled headfirst into him, knocking him away before I bared my own fangs to growl at him.

Unlike the last time I had fought with Lucius, this time I wasn't trying to just be defensive when we reared up on our hind legs and started biting and clawing at each other. For the first time I regretted the fact that I'd never taken part in the ring fights in either my pack or Jeremy's; a little experience could've gone a long way right about then. Lucius was fierce and aggressive, and I found myself dodging from his attacks more often than I wanted. Jeremy couldn't help me either, being too busy trying to ward off Riley and Ennis.

But then I got help I never saw coming. Another lupine shape came rushing in, jumping into Lucius's side with teeth bared. A smaller, thinner lupine shape, not yet fully grown. With a scent I had become very familiar with over the past few weeks.

Andrea.

Lucius had time to reel in shock from the fact that his alpha's little girl had just attacked him, before Leon suddenly stepped in, having shifted to his four-legged form and lunging at him, his fur bristling and his ears flattened back as he growled through his fangs. And by now the rest of the pack had noticed the commotion and was on their way to find out what was going on or protect their alpha, half of them already four-legged and rushing forward.

I could see Lucius looking around and taking stock of the situation. This was supposed to have been a quick there and gone job; he hadn't counted on it getting this complicated. He turned to Riley and Ennis with a quick *"buff,"* and the three of them hurriedly began retreating back to the forest.

I looked to Jeremy, contemplating whether we should go after them, when the question was taken out of our hands. Members of my former pack suddenly surrounded us, teeth bared on all sides. At first I thought we were about to be jumped, when somebody finally recognized me.

174

Charlene stepped forward out of the throng, eyes wide as she looked down at me and gasped, "Evelyn? Is that you?"

My gaze turned in the direction of Andrea, who had just heard my real name spoken by a Caldour. I was so screwed.

Resigned, I shifted form, rising up on my two legs. Jeremy and Andrea followed suit behind me. "Yes," I sighed. "It's me."

"'Evelyn?'" Andrea echoed.

My father suddenly came forward out of the crowd. "Evelyn! Where have you been? We've been looking for you for weeks!"

"Elena, what's going on?" Andrea asked.

"'Elena?'" Charlene said.

"Who are these?" Leon demanded, after shifting back to his two-legged shape. "Tell me they're not Morgandorfs!"

"You're bringing *Morgandorfs* here?" old Tobias demanded.

"Yes," I admitted. "They're Morgandorfs."

Leon grabbed me by the arm, pulling me away. "Move aside, Evelyn!" he commanded, while most of the rest of the pack advanced growling on Jeremy and Andrea.

"No, I won't!" I shouted, throwing off Leon's hand and pressing myself to Jeremy.

"Evelyn, what are you doing?" my dad demanded.

"I love him, Dad," I said. "If you want him, you have to go through me."

"'Dad?'" Andrea echoed. "This is your dad?"

I blinked, my heart sinking. "Yes."

"You're a *Caldour?*"

I lifted my head from Jeremy's chest to look at Andrea. "I told you to go back to your father! I didn't want you following me!"

A hand grabbed me by the shoulder and jerked me around, bringing me face to raging, venomous face with my dad. "Tell me this isn't true!" he demanded, practically foaming at the mouth. "We've been worried sick about you all this time, and this is where you've been? With *them*? Letting this... Morgandorf filth violate you?"

A lot of angry grumbles and curses started coming from all directions, and I heard the word "traitor" flung by a few of them.

I ignored all the barbs, and focused on my father. "At least he respects me and what I want, which is more than I can say for you, Dad."

Dad's eyes went wild and his nostrils flared, and he raised his hand up to bring it down hard across my face. Leon stepped in, catching his arm by the wrist before his hand could touch me. Leon looked me over disapprovingly, and then looked to Andrea. "The girl can go," he said.

176

"Leon!" James protested.

"She's just a kid," Leon said. "We're not barbarians." He looked to Andrea again and told her, "Run back where you belong, kid."

Andrea looked to me again, too many thoughts and emotions playing across her face for me to peg any one down. But finally she shifted to her four-legged shape and dashed through the crowd surrounding us, which parted to let her disappear into the woods.

Then Leon's attention turned to Jeremy, whom he pointed a finger at. "Lock that one in the shed until we figure out what to do with him."

"No!" I shouted.

Leon's gaze whirled on me, and his hand lashed out to grab my arm, yanking me away from Jeremy. "*You* are going to stay in your house until I say otherwise!"

"Let go of me!"

"If I have to have somebody nail your windows shut I will!" He lifted his head and pointed to Jeremy. "Take him away!"

A couple of my packmates came and took hold of Jeremy's arms and started pulling him away. I continued fighting against Leon's grip—and when he didn't release me, I suddenly turned vicious.

With my arm still in his grasp, I shifted to my four-legged form right there, lunging up and clawing at him, very nearly getting my jaws around his face before he recoiled and released me. As soon as I had four paws on the ground I turned and leapt for the two holding Jeremy.

I knew these two guys. I'd known them all my life. Dane used to play with me when I was little, and he always made the best steaks of anyone in the pack. Garth liked to serenade us all with the sweetest music on his guitar. But right then none of that mattered, so long as they had their hands on Jeremy. I jumped on Garth, locking my jaws around his neck just enough to draw blood; if I'd closed my teeth any tighter I could've ripped his throat out. When Garth dropped on his back, I lunged and snapped at Dane, who backed away, letting Jeremy go.

As soon as Jeremy's arms were free, he dropped to all fours and grew out his fur, snapping at Dane's leg and bringing Dane crashing to the ground hamstringed. With that the two of us ran toward the wall of teeth and fur surrounding us, and leaped into the air, jumping clear over the impeding lupine shapes before making our mad dash for the woods.

CHAPTER EIGHT

We knew we were being pursued this time. We could clearly hear multiple sets of running paws chasing behind us. We ducked and jumped and weaved about, navigating the forest in the most erratic patterns we could, trying everything we could think of to lose our pursuers.

Even after we could no longer hear them running after us, we still didn't slow down. We knew they would still be able to follow our scent trail; we could only hope that they would decide to back off once they realized the trail was leading them straight to the Morgandorf village.

We weren't really thinking about what would be waiting for us once we got there.

We finally emerged from the trees into Jeremy's village—and skidded to a stop at the sight of the whole pack gathered around with heavy, angry looks, which they all lifted to look at us when we arrived. At the center of it all, looking right at us with a smug grin, was Lucius.

We assumed our two-legged shapes and stood before the crowd, exchanging serious looks with each other. Both of us knew we were in deep shit. "I can explain…" I began.

Ricardo appeared out of the crowd, stepping up to us with urgency. "Jeremy, is it true?" he demanded.

"Ricardo…" Jeremy tried weakly.

"*Is it true?* Have you been harboring a Caldour right in our midst this whole time?"

Jeremy didn't say anything. Ricardo's look and several of the others' turned to me.

I set my jaw and told them all, "I only lied to you all about my name and where I came from. My real name is Evelyn Godfrey. And yes, I was born to the Caldour pack. Everything else you know about me is true. I was arranged to be married to my alpha, Leon Caldour. I ran away from my pack to escape that arrangement, and to be with Jeremy."

Ricardo looked all kinds of unhappy. And looking at the faces of the pack I could see a whole rainbow of negative emotions among them. Anger. Shock. Betrayal. Hatred. Disbelief.

"What are we standing around for?" someone shouted. "She's a Caldour! You know what we should do!"

"She turned her back on them!" someone else said. "Doesn't that count for something?"

"Once a Caldour, always a Caldour!"

"She's our friend!" That was Tara who said that.

"She was never our friend!" someone said. "She lied to us! She's a stranger!"

"If she'd told us she was a Caldour from the beginning, we would've chased her away! What choice did she have?"

"I don't care why she did it! I'll never, *never* trust a Caldour! And this only proves we can't trust her!"

"Everyone, enough!" Ricardo commanded. "Elena… Evelyn… whatever your name is… I understand your reasoning. Given your situation, I'm sure many of us might have done the same. But ultimately, you still belong to an enemy pack, and whether you still want to belong to them or not, your ties to them cannot be completely severed. Like it or not, you're a beacon for trouble that I can't ask my pack to take on."

"But Daddy!" Andrea's voice spoke up, as she appeared out of the crowd, approaching her father. "What has she ever done to hurt us?"

"I'm sorry, Andie. Even if she really means us no harm, the rest of her pack, who knows she's been here now, certainly does. They'll come looking for her."

"Then we could protect her!" Andrea whimpered.

"And how long do you think this pack will accept her?" Ricardo said. "Knowing she's a Caldour, who's to say they won't butcher her in her sleep?"

"*You* are!" Andrea insisted. "You're the alpha! You can forbid anyone from touching her!"

Ricardo sighed. "Andie, you have a big heart. And I'm proud of that. But a Caldour can never be welcome among us."

My head hung in dismay. "We could have run away together," I told them. "We were tempted to do that, even. To get away from all the fighting, the hate, the anger… but we came back. We wanted to put an end to this feud, before anyone else either of us cared about got hurt, or worse."

"Big dreams," one of the pack named Cole said. "It's easier said than done. There's no making peace with a pack of killers and thieves."

"Your pack killed three of my family," said the one named Ethan. "Including my mother!"

"The Caldours are more like hyenas than wolves!" said someone else. "They take whatever they want, they kill for fun and they laugh about it!"

"You know, a lot of the wolves in my pack say the same things about you," I told them all. "All my life I've been told the Morgandorfs are bloodthirsty, slavering beasts who would steal our homes and slaughter our pups if given the chance!"

Brock suddenly lunged forward angrily, forcing someone to grab him and hold him back. "Say that again, you Caldour scum!" he spat.

"It's just what they say," I said. "The point is, I never cared about any of that. It never mattered to me that Jeremy was a Morgandorf, any more than it mattered to him that I was a Caldour. If we can love each other, why can't the rest of us?"

"Yeah, Dad!" Andrea protested. "Isn't she proof that everything we've ever been told about the Caldours is wrong?"

"One she-wolf doesn't erase generations of bloodshed," Cole argued. "There's a mountain of Morgandorf corpses standing between us and any chance of peace."

"Is Russell one of them?" I ventured to ask.

That gave them a moment's pause. "Leonard thinks Russell's going to pull through," Ricardo said.

"Can't we treat that as a start?" Jeremy offered.

"Oh, sure," Regan muttered. "Let's go thank the Caldours for only *nearly* killing our packmate. We'll give them a big gift basket and invite them to barbecues so they can *FINISH THE DAMN JOB!*"

Ricardo looked at me levelly, tempering down whatever prejudices he might have had much better than most of the rest of the pack were doing. "Your intentions are noble, and I can certainly appreciate them. And I wish it were as easy as you want it to be. But there is too much history to overcome. And I'm afraid I can no longer afford to shelter you." He looked to Jeremy and added, "Either of you."

Tara turned a worried look to Ricardo. "What are you saying?"

Ricardo lifted a finger to point at Jeremy and me. "The both of you are banished from this pack!" he declared.

"Ricardo, no!" Laura protested, stepping up by her husband's side and taking him by the shoulder. "Not both of them! Jeremy's one of us!"

"He threw that away!" someone in the crowd spat.

"He never should've touched that Caldour bitch!"

"He's a disgrace to the Morgandorf pack!"

"Everyone, calm down!" Tara spoke up. "We don't want to condemn one of our own just for choosing to love someone, even if she is a Caldour!"

"Speak for yourself!" someone said. "He's a fucking traitor for not killing her the moment he saw her!"

"Yeah! He brought that filth here! Among us! Shared our food, our houses with her... banishment's too good a punishment!"

The level of hate suddenly being spewed at me was enough to make me recoil.

"Now that's enough!" Ricardo shouted. "I have spoken! Banishment it is!"

Jeremy and I looked about uncomfortably, before Ricardo finally said, "I suggest you leave now, while I can still hold them back."

I exchanged another look with Jeremy, before we despondently turned and started heading back into the forest. We'd barely taken three steps when Andrea shouted, "Wait!" I turned to see her running for me, grabbing me by the wrist and looking up at me with tear-filled eyes.

"I'm sorry, Andie," I said softly. "I'll miss you."

Helplessly, Andrea let my arm slip from her grasp, still holding her hands up in the position where they held me as Jeremy and I shifted to our four-legged forms and loped off into the woods.

*

We ran a short distance into the forest when I pulled up short, catching a scent on the air. Jeremy paused beside me, not sure at first what was up, until he sniffed the air and caught it too. I could clearly make out the scents of Corey, Marla, Jana and Rudy from my pack; they were on our trail, looking for us.

I turned a look to Jeremy; we knew what we needed to do. I let him lead the way, him being more familiar with this area of the woods. Before long we found a stream and turned to run through it, following along its length, letting the flowing water trickle over our paws, washing our scents downstream.

After splashing through the stream for a good distance, we continued on away from where we'd been, running aimlessly into the woods. We just kept on running with no goal in sight, until we exhausted ourselves and trotted to a stop.

We came to a rest at last on top of a hill beneath a tree, where I collapsed down in a dejected heap as I shifted to my two-legged form. My eyes squeezed shut, forcing out the tears I'd been holding in. And once I let them out, they would not stop. I was too busy crying into the dirt to even notice when Jeremy shifted form and knelt beside me and started rubbing my shoulders.

"Hey," he said, pulling me up and into his arms. "Come on. It's okay. I'm here."

"We failed them," I sobbed. "Our families. We were supposed to stop the fighting… we couldn't stop anything!"

Jeremy leaned back against the tree, cradling me in his arms. "It's like Ricardo said: a pack can only be led where they want to go. The two of us were never going to undo generations of hate and violence all by ourselves."

"So there's nothing we can do?" I choked.

Jeremy looked a little glum. "Maybe there isn't. Maybe we'll just have to accept that this feud is bigger than us."

"Don't say that!" I sobbed.

"I know it's not easy. But we may have to get used to it. Your pack tried to lock us up; mine drove us away. What is there left for us to do for them? They don't want our help."

I buried my face in his chest. I couldn't think of anything else to say to him. So I just rested there, crying it out against him.

"So I guess we're left with what we wanted to do before," he said. "We run away. We put this conflict as far behind us as we can, and we never look back. We start our own life together. No pack, no alphas, no war. We get a place all our own, and we have our own pups, who never hear the names 'Caldour' or 'Morgandorf.' Whatever we want, with no one to say no."

I had to admit, that did sound like a good plan. It may not have been the outcome I was really hoping for, but it was something I could get behind easily. I lifted my head from his chest to look at his face. "I think I like that."

He reached a hand up and brought his thumb to my face, wiping my tears away from my eyes. He bent his head down, and I brought mine up to accept his kiss. My hand came up to grip him by the back of his neck, holding onto him with all the passion I had as I melded into his kiss; at this point, Jeremy was all I had.

I climbed up into his lap, embracing him fully, my lips never leaving his. My breath was his, and his was mine. Our pressing flesh was as one. My hips churned back and forth in his lap, rubbing my crotch against his flaccid member, working it up and getting it nice and hard for me.

We stayed like that for a long time, just making out under that tree, my hips gyrating in his lap. I think I may have even gotten off once or twice just from rubbing against him before I even put him inside me. Ultimately, we were at that long enough that we ended up needing very little foreplay. He bent and kissed my tits a little, and felt up my butt, but that was about it before I finally lifted my hips up, angled him toward my opening, and sat back down.

At that point, I rested my head on his shoulder and just settled for humping up and down on his lap. I didn't make any big thrashing motions or loud moans; I just moved rhythmically and breathed heavy a lot. I clutched at his back while he clutched at mine, hoping we would never have to let each other go.

I found myself thinking back to that night in his room, the night we realized that Lucius was onto us. I recalled how I'd wished we could have stayed forever in that room. I still wished that. I wanted us to be back in that room again. And I wanted us to never have to leave it. Everything he'd talked about: no packs, no alphas, no feud… if the world beyond those four walls could have just not existed, if Jeremy and I could be the only people, human or wolf in the world… nothing could have made me happier.

We both came softly like that, and then went for two more rounds, once doggy style and once with him on top. After that point, we finally tired ourselves out, and spooned up together lying in the dirt.

I fell asleep dreaming of the future Jeremy had described. We could live in town, near the edge of the forest. I could go to a local college, and pursue an actual career, without being an alpha's trophy wife. Jeremy could work for a construction company, coming home glistening with sweat in a muscle shirt, making me want to just rip it off him and smother myself in those shiny muscles. We could have three beautiful pups; two girls and a boy, whom we could take into the woods in the back yard, and let them run around in their four-legged forms and chase rabbits and butterflies. We wouldn't even need a pack; what good had a pack ever done for us?

It was a lovely dream. And it didn't feel out of reach, either. It could be the simplest dream in the world to achieve, couldn't it?

I wanted to believe. I wanted to think that Jeremy and I could be happy.

And I kept thinking we would be until the moment I awoke.

I was still sleeping peacefully in my blissful fantasy when I was roughly jerked awake by something grabbing me by the arms and pulling. My eyes snapped open, looking up to the faces of my own packmates. Marla and Corey were there, yanking me up to my feet, Marla holding my wrists together and starting to bind them, while Corey held my torso in place. Behind me, Rudy and Jana were busy tying Jeremy by his wrists to the tree.

"What are you doing?" I shouted.

"We're taking you back where you belong," Marla said. "And we're leaving that Morgandorf scum here where he can't get his filthy hands on you anymore!"

"No! Let go of me!"

"She doesn't want to go with you!" Jeremy shouted. "Don't you see that?"

"Hold her!" Corey called. Rudy and Jana finished what they were doing with Jeremy and came to grab me by the arms, holding me steady for Marla to finish tying me.

Once my hands were bound, Corey grabbed me by them and pulled me roughly to him, while Marla marched over to Jeremy with a look of righteous anger on her face. "I don't think what she wants is what's good for her anymore, Morgandorf!"

she spat. "If what she wants is to run away from the pack that raised her to be with a drooling, pup-eating, sodomizing sack of shit like you, then you'd better believe we're gonna do something to stop her! Now you just sit there while we take her home, and hope your own kind comes and gets you out of there before some rabid weasel comes along and eats your junk off. And personally, I'm gonna be rooting for the latter option." And then she spat in Jeremy's face, making him flinch.

"Let's go," Jana said, and they started back home, pulling me helplessly along behind them as I could only look back and watch as Jeremy slowly shrank in to the distance behind me, straining futilely against his bonds.

It took hours of me staggering along behind them before we finally made it back to our village; a lot longer than it would have taken us on four legs, but that would have made it a lot harder for them to drag me there. As soon as we emerged from the trees, Corey threw his head back and howled for the rest of the pack, who promptly came rushing toward us. "We got her," Marla announced.

As a crowd gathered to meet us, Leon appeared, stepping forward to take me from Rudy. He looked at me with a heavy brow and a hard-set mouth, his disappointment with me pouring from him like smoke from a chimney. "You've put us through a lot of grief, Evelyn," he grumbled. "First we thought you'd run away just to spite us. For a while we even thought the Morgandorfs had killed you." His mouth curled into a hideous, hateful snarl as he said, "But to find out you'd abandoned us to *be* with one of them… you couldn't have cut us more deeply!"

I met his gaze with a calm scowl. "I guess that means you don't want me for your wife anymore. Maybe that was what I wanted."

Leon's teeth clenched in anger—and his hand came up and swatted me hard across the face. As I recoiled from the blow and blinked my eyes open again, I saw a flash of remorse running across his face, and he took a step back. "I'm sorry I had to do that," he said. "I suggest you don't make me do it again."

"I didn't know I could make my alpha do anything he didn't want to," I said, undeterred.

I could see I'd ruffled him again, but he held himself back from hitting me this time. "You've picked up some sass. Something your Morgandorf hosts must have taught you, I'm betting. I'm going to make sure to fix that."

I didn't reply this time, except to continue giving him a defiant glare.

"Where is she?" I heard Dad's voice then. He appeared pushing his way through the crowd, stopping short when he found me. And he didn't look any happier than Leon.

"Hi, Dad," I muttered, sounding bitter.

Without another word, he grabbed me by the arm and began pulling me back toward our house. "No! Dad, let go of me!"

He still said nothing, continuing to yank me roughly along, past the horrified face of my mother, in through our front door and down into the basement, where he shoved me forward, forcing me to descend the stairs. At that point he finally unbound my hands, and shoved me down against the wall.

"I've been disappointed with you before, Evelyn," he said. "And I've been mad at you plenty of times. But now... I'm actually ashamed of you! You turned your back on everything your mother and I taught you, *everything* you were brought up to believe in... for a filthy, scum-sucking Morgandorf!"

"It's not like that, Dad!" I protested. "Jeremy's a good man! He's never done anything to hurt me, and he—"

"Now that's enough!" Dad snapped at me. "You are going to stay down here until you learn a lesson, missy."

"Dad, please!"

"Don't force me to chain you to the wall!"

I stopped talking after that.

Dad started marching up the stairs, while I stepped up to the bottom of them, with him blocking the only way I had of getting out. "I'll bring you something to eat later. You'll be cared for. But until you remember what it means to be a Caldour, you're not going anywhere."

And with that, he stepped out, shutting the door behind him, and I heard the lock latch. In spite of myself, I ran up the stairs to grab the doorknob, already knowing it was useless. I fiddled helplessly with the stubborn knob, and pounded once on the door, before I collapsed to my knees and began to cry.

CHAPTER NINE

The pups were starting to play a little rough. It had been amusing at first, watching them jump and tumble around with that squeaky little rubber alien with the big googly eyes, but now two of them had the squeak toy in their jaws and were playing a little tug-o-war with it, threatening to tear it in two, while the third was eagerly coming up to snatch it away from both of them.

It was at that point that I decided to step in and mediate the game. "Hey, now," I said, getting up from my lawn chair and stepping over to them. "If you can't play nice, I'm going to have to take your toys away. No more fighting," I said as I knelt down and took hold of the little green thing in their jaws, which they calmly released and let me take, looking up at me with meek eyes. "What did I tell you all?"

At that question, the three little furry, four-legged creatures before me rose up on their hind legs, which began extending into human legs. Their shoulders reconfigured to allow their front legs to move to the sides and reshape into human arms. Their fur disappeared to reveal human skin, and their little snouts shrank away, as the faces of three little children emerged on them, standing naked before me with humbled looks.

"Fighting is bad," said the seven-year-old girl with the little brown curls. "Fighting gets people hurt."

"That's right, Lisa," I nodded. "And what do people who fight get?"

"No dessert," said all three of them in the same monotone expression.

"That's right!" I said, pointing a finger at them. "So what are you all going to do now?"

"Play nice," they drawled.

"Very good," I smiled. "Maybe I should get some more toys out for each of you, so you don't have to fight over them. Is that okay?"

The kids smiled and nodded. "I want my sparkly ball, mommy!" said little four-year-old Audrey.

"I'm gonna get my Nerf gun!" said six-year-old Cody.

"Only if you don't shoot your sisters with it," I said.

As the pups ran to retrieve their playthings, I lifted my head and sniffed the air, catching Jeremy's scent approaching. I turned around to see him appearing from around the house, which prompted the youngest of the pups to suddenly change direction and come running for him. "Daddy!" Audrey cheered, opening her arms to him as he bent to pick her up.

"Hey, there!" he beamed. "How's daddy's little bumper?"

"Mommy take me swimming today!" she chirped. "I swim better than Cody!"

"You do?" he grinned.

"She's lying!" Cody protested. "She didn't want to go in!"

"I swim good!" little Audrey insisted.

"I'm sure you do, sweetie," he nodded, setting her back down. "Why don't you go play some more, and let me talk to mommy."

Our little girl ran off to join her brother and sister, while Jeremy stepped up and greeted me with a short, chaste kiss. "She only got in the water for about two minutes," I whispered to him. "But she was really proud of herself when she did. I may have let her embellish the story a little." Jeremy chuckled, and slipped an arm around my waist, pressing himself to my side as we watched the kids playing some more.

Eventually we started up the steps to the back door, while I called to the kids to say, "Keep playing nice, pups. Remember, Mommy knows!"

"Yes, Mom," they drawled.

We moved through the back door into the kitchen, and I shut the door behind us to say, "My father doesn't know if he'll be able to make it to our Thanksgiving feast," I said.

"Is his health any better?" Jeremy asked.

"Mom says he's up and moving again, but she's keeping him on a strict low-sodium diet. And apparently she's facing a daily struggle keeping him from working himself too hard."

"You sure he's not still just trying to spite me?" Jeremy offered, his head tilting. "You know he's never been too happy about you marrying a Morgandorf, even after our packs made peace."

I smiled, and shook my head. "Trust me, he's over that by now. Believe me, I've worried about it often enough to check."

"Well that's good to hear," he said, taking me into his arms. "Andrea's a sure thing, though. She can't wait to see the pups again."

I grinned wider. "Oh, and they're even more excited to see their 'Auntie Andie.'"

Jeremy rolled his eyes with a dry smirk. "I still think that sounds like a stutter."

"But the pups just love calling her that," I said. "And I get why."

"Well," he said, getting a wicked twinkle in his eye, "there's a few things I think I'd enjoy calling you tonight."

I narrowed my eyes and smirked at him. "Are you thinking dirty thoughts again?"

"With you? Always."

I giggled and kissed him.

This was it. This was what I always wanted. Life couldn't have turned out any more perfect than this. After all the pain we'd endured, all the fear of losing each other, of losing our families to the war between our packs, of being forced into marriages with people we didn't love, we'd ultimately gotten everything we could have dreamed for.

I had Jeremy. I had my pups. I had my happy life.

I held onto Jeremy tightly as I kissed him, as if I wanted to make sure he never slipped away.

And then in the next moment, he did.

He was suddenly gone from my arms, his body removed from my touch, his lips disappearing from my kiss. I opened my eyes to find him simply gone, leaving no trace. I reached out to grab at the air where he had just been, but nothing was there to grab at but air. Suddenly panicked, I looked out the window where my pups should have been playing, only to see them fade away like smoke. And then the walls of my house started falling away like the plywood walls of a cheap film set, disappearing into shadows and mist, until all around me was nothing but darkness.

"No!" I cried to the void. "Give them back! Please!"

But there was nothing out there to give a response. My perfect life had simply evaporated, replaced with a great black hole of nothingness.

But no… there was something there.

I heard Leon's voice echoing in the darkness. "It will never be yours," he thundered. "You'll always be mine. The only future you have is what I give you."

"No! It's my future! You can't take that from me!"

I saw Leon's proud face, with his dark eyes and his slicked-back hair, looking back at me from the darkness, shaking his head. "Nothing you have is yours. I'll always be there. Everywhere."

And then he was reaching out to me. But it was like his hand was enormous, getting bigger and bigger the closer it came to me, as if it was all around me, encompassing everything. There was nowhere I could go where I wouldn't be in his grasp. No matter what I did, I would always be in the palm of his hand.

And now his hand was closing around me.

My world was encroaching on me with his grip. I curled up, bringing my knees up to my chest, holding my hands up to my sides as my space to move grew tighter and ever tighter. I started gasping for air; it was getting harder for me to breathe. Before long, there was nothing left in the world but Leon's hand, wrapped around me, and beginning to squeeze…

I heard the sound of a door opening. I blinked my eyes open and lifted my head off the cold floor beneath me. As my vision slowly cleared, my surroundings became familiar again. I was still in the basement where Dad had locked me, curled up naked on the floor against the wall. Soft sunlight was streaming in through the narrow window up at the top of the wall to my right. And I heard the sounds of my dad's footsteps descending the stairs to my left.

He appeared coming around the end of the stairs, holding a steaming bowl of pasta in his hands. "You hungry?" he said.

I didn't answer verbally. I just silently glared at him. It was how I had regarded him ever since he put me down here. I'd lost track of how many days it had been by now. There were no clocks down here; the only way to track the passage of time was by the daylight coming in through that little window.

Dad had gotten used to my cold, silent stares by now. He kept hoping I'd open up to him this time, but so far it hadn't happened. "Still nothing?" he said.

I kept quiet again.

"Fine then," he said, and set the bowl down in front of me. "I can keep waiting for you to come around. You're not going anywhere."

He got up and started back toward the stairs. As I saw his back shrinking away from me, I finally decided to open my mouth and say something to him. "Are you enjoying this?"

With his hand on the rail, he turned look at me earnestly. "Not for a second. Despite what you might think of me right now, you're the most important thing in the world to me. That's why your betrayal stings me so deeply. And that's why I have to resort to these measures."

"If you really cared about me, Dad, you'd have respected my choices and what I wanted, instead of trying to make all my choices for me."

Dad frowned at me. "I want what's best for you, Evelyn. Sometimes that means having to administer some tough love, when your choices are leading you down a bad path." He started back up the stairs again. "I'll be back to check on you again later."

After the door shut behind him, I poked absently at the bowl of curled noodles in front of me with the fork that stuck out the top of them. I wasn't that hungry just now. I hadn't felt all that hungry for a long time, honestly. Yes, I ate the food that Dad always brought down to me. Eventually. But in the time I'd been down here, I was guessing I'd probably lost at least three pounds already.

I pushed the bowl aside and got up, and walked to that little window. I had to get up on my tiptoes to see through it, and even then the angle didn't allow me much of a view. I could see several members of my pack going about their business, some of whom I couldn't see well enough to identify, and I couldn't get their scents from down in there either. But I could see some of my old friends going about their day. I saw Charlene talking with Becky and Trina out by the circle, and I could see Terry's rusty pickup driving through the village, still alive and sputtering as it returned from town. I could see several members of the pack going about in their four-legged forms, sitting about sphinx-like or trotting into the village with fresh-killed meat in their jaws. And I could see Leon leaning against a wall, talking shop with James and old Tobias.

My pack. My friends and family. The wolves who had been part of my life for as long as I had lived.

And now I was a prisoner to them.

A pair of small, feminine feet walked by the window in front of my face, and then stopped. She bent down to look at me, revealing the face of sixteen-year-old Samantha, one of the growing pups in our pack. I smiled softly. "Hi, Sam," I said.

She looked back at me blankly for a moment—and then hawked and spit a big gob of loogie at the glass in front of me, making me recoil.

Then she got up and continued on her way.

*

Time moved at a snail's pace in that basement. The only things I had to keep me company were that window, the occasional meals that Dad brought me, and a bucket to do my business in. So long, long hours were spent just pacing around or sitting in the corner.

I slept a lot while I was in there. With nothing else to do, I ended up nodding off pretty frequently, curled up against the wall. And honestly, I liked sleeping down there. Sleep was my only means of escape. For brief periods I could forget about where I was, and I could dream about still being with Jeremy.

I dreamed we were still back in his room in the Morgandorf village, where we had all our best sex in the comfort of his bed, cradling each other in our arms, with four walls to separate the rest of the world from us. I dreamed we were back out in the forest, just the two of us, running about in our four-legged forms, hunting and eating raw meat and sleeping under the stars. I dreamed I was still Elena the stray, living as a guest of the Morgandrof pack, making friends with all of them, swimming in their lake and joining Andrea for more of her teenage hijinks. I dreamed of a time when there was no conflict between our packs, when we could come and go as we pleased, when no one would threaten us and tell us we were wrong. I dreamed I could introduce Jeremy to Mom and Dad, and they would smile and shake his hand and invite him over for dinner and cherry pie. And I dreamed some more about that beautiful house we might have, and those three beautiful pups, and that beautiful life together.

But invariably I would always wake up, and I would be back to that dingy, lonely, stinky basement, locked away from all of that.

When I woke up again, the half-eaten pasta still sat in front of me, having long since grown cold. I had no idea if another day had passed or if it was just later on the same day. I rarely did anymore.

I heard the door open again, and immediately thought that Dad was coming back to check on me again. But the footsteps I heard coming down the stairs were lighter than Dad's heavy footfalls. And it wasn't his scent that I smelled approaching.

Instead it was Mom's. She appeared leaning cautiously around the end of the stairs to see me. "Evelyn?" she said.

I didn't say anything at first. I blinked a couple of times, not entirely sure at first that she was really there. She hadn't visited me once in however long it had been since Dad threw me down here; what had suddenly changed? Or was the isolation finally getting to me?

But I finally decided she was real when she walked toward me, knelt down and placed a gentle hand on my head. "How are you doing?"

I could only respond by giving her a look that silently said, "How the hell do you *think* I'm doing?"

She frowned, and sighed. "I'm sorry about this. I really am. The worst thing in the world when you're a parent is to see your child in pain."

"Then why are you letting Dad do this to me?"

Mom grimaced uncomfortably. "I wish I could do something to help you. But it's not just your father I'd be going against. Leon is also sanctioning this. If I let you out, he would severely punish us both."

I laid my face down in my arms, getting that feeling of helplessness that had become so familiar lately.

"I came down here because I want to try to understand. I want to know what you were thinking this whole time."

I lifted my head, giving my mother a nasty look. "I was thinking I found someone who made me feel like I was in a romance novel or John Hughes movie. Remember you saying something about that, when we were talking about my engagement to Leon?"

Mom paused. "I remember telling you that love wasn't always like those things. I said it didn't always happen in one big moment, and that it takes time to build."

"But sometimes it *is* like that, isn't it?" I said. "And you can still build it after that, can't you?"

Mom looked uncomfortable. "Evelyn... I know it's easy to think you're in love with dangerous boys when you're young, but it's not real—"

"Mom, shut up!"

She blinked, jerking her head back in surprise.

"You don't know anything! Jeremy is the least dangerous guy I've ever known! If anything, Leon is way more dangerous than he is! He's never been anything but good to me! He actually listens to me, which is more than I can say of anyone here. And he protected me when someone else tried to hurt me. It's not just some thrill I get by running around with a forbidden lover! It's real with him!"

Mom looked like she was about to cry out of pity. "Evelyn... did you ever think that maybe he was just using you? It's what a Morgandorf would do."

"That's all that matters to you, isn't it?" I snapped. "That he's a Morgandorf. You think that's all you need to know about him. You think they're all the same. We've all demonized them, and made them out to be killers and thieves. Well you know what? They say the same things about us. You should've heard some of the things they accused the Caldour pack of while I was there! Out of the mouths of their pups even! I mean it was like being in a mirror world over there. They all live just like we do. They have families that love each other just like us. And their pups are beautiful. Just like ours. If you'd just give them a chance, you'd see there's nothing to hate about them at all!"

Mom looked like she didn't know what to say anymore. "I... well... you..."

"Now everyone's treating me like a traitor, because I couldn't bring myself to love someone who treated me like a trophy, who told me he was going to marry me like it was a done deal and never bothered to ask what I wanted, and instead I chose to love someone who actually respected me, instead of hating him just because he was born to the wrong pack."

"Evelyn..."

"When Dad and Leon made that whole arrangement, you told me I should just accept it and learn to like it. So that Dad could use me to bandage his wounded pride, and so Leon could have me as a prize. You tried to tell me there was nothing I could do but accept that their needs were more important than mine. That's what Dad thinks being loyal to him means; he wants me to put my wants aside for his. Well, I'm sorry, Mom, but I don't accept that!"

Mom just looked all kinds of uncomfortable. "Evelyn, please listen..."

"If you're not gonna let me out of here, then just go away!"

Mom tried reaching out to touch my shoulder. I scowled and slapped her hand away. "JUST GET OUT!"

There was nothing more she could say, and it seemed like she finally realized that. With a pitiful expression on her face, she finally stood up and backed away toward the stairs, pausing to look at me sadly before ascending back into the house.

Once she was gone I curled up on the floor and laid my head back down.

CHAPTER TEN

I was pretty sure it was a few hours later, judging by the window showing night outside, when I was roused from a state of semi-consciousness by the sound of muffled voices yelling above me. It was hard to make out words through the walls surrounding me, but I could recognize the voices as belonging to my parents.

I got up and climbed the stairs, pressing my ear to the locked door. "Rene, the only thing you're accomplishing is making her hate you!"

"Maybe that's true," Dad said. "Maybe she'll hate me now, but she'll thank us later, when she learns her lesson."

"What lesson is that? That you're always right? That Leon is always right?"

"That she owes this pack her loyalty, and that running off with Morgandorfs is betraying us!"

"Rene, this is cruel!"

"Any crueler than what she did to us? Disappearing for weeks and then turning up with one of them?"

"Yes! It is crueler than that! She's been down there four days; she's probably losing her mind by now!"

Four days? Was that all it had been? It felt like I'd been in that basement for a lot longer than that. It felt like I'd been down there for weeks.

"Don't you remember how you were losing your mind while she was gone?" Dad said. "We thought she was dead somewhere, most likely mounted up as some sick trophy for the Morgandorfs to spit on! And then she comes back, and we find out she was alive all this time, and living with them by choice! If that's not enough to make you go out of your mind, I don't know what is!"

"Rene, she's young! She's following her heart! Is this really an appropriate punishment for that?"

"That sounds romantic to you, doesn't it? 'She's just following her heart.' Well she has to learn there are consequences to that!"

"But locking her in the basement? Never even letting her see daylight? Like she's some kind of criminal?"

"She *is* a criminal!" Dad suddenly blurted out. "Don't you get that? She abandoned us to consort with the Morgandorfs! Can you think of a worse crime a Caldour can commit?"

"You don't think for one second you might have pushed her away?"

"Oh, Brenda! I can't believe you're defending this!"

"I'm not condoning what she did, Rene. But you're taking this way too far!"

"Well, it doesn't matter what you think now," Dad sighed. "Leon wants her to stay down there until she comes to her senses."

"She's going to *lose* her senses down there!" Mom insisted.

"Maybe that's what it'll take!"

"Oh, my god, Rene, listen to yourself! What are you expecting her to say that'll get you to let her out of there! You think locking her up will make her stop loving that boy, and want to marry Leon? All she's going to want is to get as far away from this place as she can, if this is how we're treating her!"

"If you want to take it up with Leon, be my guest. Otherwise, she's not going anywhere."

I heard a door open, and footsteps walking through them. Then I heard Mom calling, "Rene! Rene, come back here!" And then I heard the door shut, and Mom sighed in defeat, pulled out a chair and sat down hard.

I did similarly, sinking to my knees on the step and setting my head against the door. At least Mom seemed to be more-or-less on my side, but she was outvoted. She couldn't help me even if she wanted to—and I got the sense she really did want to.

I didn't even notice at first when I started crying. It wasn't until a teardrop fell on my thigh that I realized it. I spent a few more minutes kneeling there on the step, letting all my tears out—

—before I heard my mother's footsteps approaching the door.

Just as I lifted my head, I heard the latch start to unlock and the door swung open, spilling a flood of light into the gloomy basement. I blinked at the sudden brightness, looking up to see Mom looking down at me. "Evelyn… did you hear that?"

I didn't answer her. At the moment, I was much more preoccupied with the fact that I could see the inside of the house beyond her. The clean, well-lit, comfortable house, and the outside world beyond it that had been shielded from me all this time. Something primal in me took over, as I suddenly shifted to my four-legged form and lunged forward, desperately trying to take this opportunity for freedom that had presented itself to me.

But Mom was a little quicker, swooping down and catching me in her arms, and holding on tight as I desperately struggled to get away. My claws scrabbled at the floor, and I kept whimpering like a puppy, as Mom kept grabbing me again each time I managed to slip through her grasp a little further. She repeatedly shouted my name, and told me again and again to calm down and be still.

After a minute or two I finally did, mellowing out there on the floor, and slowly returning to my two-legged shape in her arms, where I hung limply like a ragdoll, emotionally drained. Mom lifted me up to place my head on her shoulder and softly shushed me, stroking my hair. "I'm so sorry about this, baby. I wish I could do something."

"You could let me go," I sobbed. "I'll go out that door, disappear into the forest, and never look back."

"But your father would know," she said. "And Leon would know. They'd track you down, drag you back here and do even worse than what they're doing now. Not to mention what they'd do to me."

"I don't care what they'll try to do!" I protested. "I can't stay down there anymore! I have to do something!"

"I know. This whole thing, it's just horrible! Your father has really gone too far!"

"So we shouldn't have to stand for it, Mom! That's what I've been trying to say; we should be trying to change things! We shouldn't be fighting the Morgandorfs! And I shouldn't have to be locked up for trying to make that happen!"

"Evelyn…"

"What is going on here?" I heard Leon's voice demand. We looked up to the open back door to see Dad and Leon standing there, looking at us with angry eyes.

"Rene, what are you…?" Mom said. "I thought you…"

"We could hear the racket the two of you made clear across the village!" Dad said. "Why is she out of the basement?"

"Rene, please! Can't you see this has gone far enough?"

Leon scowled, and marched toward us, roughly shoving Mom away from me and grabbing me by the wrist. "Deal with your wife, Rene," he ordered.

"Nooooo!" I screeched as Leon dragged me bumping along back down the stairs into the basement. When we reached the bottom the flung me sliding across the floor to slam into the wall.

When I lifted my head again, he knelt down in front of me, getting right up in my face, all fire, brimstone, and spittle. "You think this treatment is bad?" he thundered. "My father would have had the pack rip you to pieces for consorting with that dreg-of-the-earth Morgandorf scum! Be thankful that I still care enough about you to give you a chance for redemption! Once you say to me that you recognize how you betrayed us, and that you are ready to rejoin us, and are prepared to kill the next Morgandorf you see—and make me believe it—then you may leave this basement. Not before. And if you try to get out before that again, I will personally lock you in a much smaller space, with not even the amount of sunlight you get in here, and the only food you will get is a tiny bowl of gruel once a day, and I will leave you in there, day, after day, after day, until you are so desperate for a breath of fresh air that you are willing to lick the mud from my shoes if I tell you to! Am I perfectly clear?"

I looked Leon straight in the eye—and then I gave him my answer.

I spat in his eye.

Leon recoiled, his eyes wide with shock. The alpha was always supposed to be respected and obeyed; for someone to defy him this bluntly was completely unprecedented. He blinked repeatedly as he wiped his eye, staring at me as if I had just spat fire. It was like he had no idea how to respond to this.

Except to backhand me across the face, I mean.

"One way or another, you'll learn respect again," he growled as he stood up. "If I have to beat it into you, starve you or hang you up by your toenails, I will. Remember that."

With that he started marching back up the stairs, where I now heard the indistinct sounds of my parents yelling at each other above me. I couldn't make out any words this time, and honestly, I didn't want to.

Largely because whatever they were arguing about, it sounded like Dad was winning.

Then Leon shut and locked the basement door behind him, muffling the sounds of my parents' voices, throwing me back into my terrible isolation.

*

I couldn't begin to guess how many more days I was down there. Dad's was the only face I saw for a long while; he would come down periodically, bring me some food and water, and ask if I was ready to "see reason" yet. Which of course meant he wanted me to say all the hateful propaganda Leon had told me I should say. Well, I was lonely and miserable down there, but I wasn't to that point yet. So I would take the provisions he brought me, and either keep silent, give him a nasty look, or find some way or other of generally telling him to fuck off.

I started to wonder why Mom hadn't come down to see me again. I kept hoping she would come back down and tell me she'd come up with some way to help me that she hadn't thought of before. But I never saw her. In fact, I didn't even hear her above me. That realization worried me. Had Leon done something to her? Had Dad? Had she paid the price for daring to try to help me?

"Deal with your wife," Leon had told Dad. What exactly had he meant by that?

As days ticked by and the question continued to haunt me, I started imagining the possibilities of what might have happened. And each thought that crossed my mind only made me feel worse. Maybe Mom had been locked up in another basement like this. Or maybe she'd been locked up in a worse place, like the shed or something, with less floor space and less sunlight like Leon had warned me about. Maybe she was being lashed or tortured. Or maybe…

Maybe I was becoming a paranoid mess.

I finally broke down and had to find out. One day after Dad brought me a simple bowl of soup, and as usual asked me if I was ready to cooperate—to which of course I still remained silent—I spoke up as he turned his back to leave. "Where's Mom? Why hasn't she come down to see me?"

Dad gave me an unhappy look. "Leon decided to punish your mother for letting you out by making her spend a week chained to a stake outside by her neck. I hope you're happy."

I wasn't sure what appalled me more: what he'd just told me, or the suggestion that I should be happy. "Can you think of a single reason I have to be happy?"

"I don't know what makes you happy anymore," Dad said. "After the way you've shamed this pack, for all I know you may think dragging your mother down with you and seeing her humiliated for it is a big hoot."

Oh, no he didn't just say that!

As he ascended the stairs I grabbed the bowl of soup in front of me and *flung* it at him, forcing him to duck as the soup went flying all over the place and the bowl shattered against the far wall. Dad looked over the mess I'd made, and said, "You're not getting another one."

"Wouldn't eat it anyway," I snarled.

He frowned, and continued marching out.

He started feeding me less after that. I think I was getting only one meal a day at that point. As much as I wanted to continue spiting him by pushing his food away, the malnutrition was starting to take its toll on me. The longer I stayed down there, the weaker I felt. I started to feel an ache inside my gut constantly, and it gradually got harder and harder even to just get myself up off the floor.

Even worse, after all that time with nothing to do and nowhere to go, it was getting steadily harder to maintain my grip on reality. Some days I would swear that rats were eating through the walls and creeping in to surround me, slowly growing in numbers until there were rats everywhere I could see, before I tried to scurry away in panic and disgust and landed with a thud on bare, rat-free floor. Other days I would feel the room starting to shake, until the house started cracking, and the ceiling collapsed and came crashing down on me—and then when I lifted my head after ducking and covering it, I would look up and see the ceiling still there, intact and with no cracks in the walls or anywhere.

Then came a day when I heard the sound of my mother's footsteps coming down the stairs. I looked up and smiled at her, relieved to finally see her returning to me. She bent down, gazing at me with a tender smile. "My poor pup," she whispered.

I reached up to touch her face—and found only empty air under my hand.

I cried especially hard that time.

I didn't know how much more of this I could take. At this rate, I was going to go completely insane if I didn't starve to death first.

And yet, I never gave Dad what he was looking for. I kept hoping he would realize that it wasn't going to happen; I would waste away in that basement before I turned on Jeremy. But apparently Dad was still clinging to the notion that I could be persuaded to change.

So long as neither of us was willing to budge, I was going to stay down there.

As I started to realize that, I began to wonder if maybe I should just say out loud what Dad wanted to hear. There was no way I could actually mean it, but maybe if he heard me say it, it might be enough to get me out of there. I could pull off a convincing lie, couldn't I? I had done it with the Morgandorf pack; they had spent weeks with me living among them, thinking I was someone I wasn't.

But Dad had a lot more reason to doubt my word than the Morgandorfs had. Hell, he'd be expecting me to suck up to him, to go through the motions of singing his song without really meaning it. So if I said it, I had to make him buy it.

I was in the process of thinking how I was going to do that one night, crouched on the floor of that basement, when I suddenly heard a distant howl come from somewhere outside.

It was an alert to the pack; something big was going down. With a surge of new strength that seemed to come from nowhere, I got up and peered out through that little window, seeing everyone running about, trying to get somewhere in a hurry. A lot of them were shifting to their four-legged shapes in the process, too. And while my view out of that window wasn't great, I could swear I saw more lupine shapes emerging from the trees.

The Morgandorfs were attacking.

All at once they were everywhere. It was like they had just appeared like a force of nature, swarming across the village. All at once, the village outside me had become engulfed in a sea of teeth, flying fur and bloodshed.

Ironically, it was my own confinement that was keeping me safe from the chaos outside.

Except that might not last for long, I soon realized, as I started hearing more chaos ensuing in the house above me. I could make out voices shouting, and lupine growls, and the sound of fighting and snapping. I couldn't follow any details; it was all such a blur. I kept trying to listen for some specific sounds that could allow me to discern what was actually going on up there.

And then it stopped. Everything went quiet. I strained my ears harder, searching for something… anything…

And then I did hear something.

I heard the door opening.

And then somebody was rushing down them. And as he stopped and stood before me, I blinked, convinced I had to be losing my mind again.

"Jeremy?" I choked.

"Come on," he said, grabbing my hand. "We've got to get out of here!"

"What's going on?"

"I followed my pack here when they decided to launch an attack. I was afraid for you. But we'd better leave before anyone else finds you!"

He started tugging at my arm. "But wait," I protested. "My family… what about them?"

"Your family locked you down here, for loving me," he pointed out. "They're not going to help you now."

I couldn't argue with that.

When he started running up the steps, this time I didn't resist him pulling me along. We reached the house above, finding it empty of anyone else, but tables and furniture had been overturned and broken, and every door was standing open. Jeremy and I promptly shifted to our four-legged shapes and went running out the front door, into the scene of chaos outside.

It was just like that night when my pack had attacked theirs. It was like I was seeing a mirror image of the same fight—but I had no intention of staying to admire it. If someone from my own pack found me, they would most likely try to throw me back into that basement. And if someone from Jeremy's pack found me... I didn't want to find out what they'd do.

So we ran. We ran like hell for the trees as fast as our four paws could carry us. We put the chaos in the village as far behind us as we could. The open night sky of the village disappeared, giving way to the deeper, darker cover of the forest. We continued running, following the trail by feel, by scent, and by sound more than sight as we dashed through the gloom, weaving past trees and jumping hills and roots.

I could swear we only ran for a short while, but when we finally stopped I knew the village was already miles behind us. And at that moment, all I could think was: *Good riddance.* My pack, which claimed to love me, which claimed I had betrayed them, had in essence betrayed me. If who I wanted to love was such a crime to them, then I decided they would no longer have my love.

Fuck them all. Let them and the Morgandorfs kill each other for all I care. I was tired of being punished for wanting my own life, or trying to make a difference.

Besides, with Jeremy here, I had everything I needed. As we settled down in that little quarry by the stream, which I realized was in that place where we first met, I made sure to let him know that. It was ironic that I waited until we had shifted back to our two-legged forms before I pounced on him. "I was beginning to think I'd never see you again," I breathed as I repeatedly kissed him. "I thought I was gonna shrivel up and die down there!"

"Don't you have more faith in me than that?" he said, in between kissing me back. "Nothing on this Earth could keep me away from you."

We rolled about in the dirt, our hands roving all over each other and our feet kicking everywhere. I felt up the muscles of his back and the firmness of his butt, while he palmed my breasts and suckled on my neck. I ground my crotch against him as he kissed along my collarbone, taking my tits into his mouth, making me quiver and moan.

Yes… yes… after so long… finally!

"Evie?"

I stared up into Jeremy's face. "I missed you so much," I breathed. "I almost went crazy without you."

"I'm here now," he said, his erection rubbing against the top of my thigh, making my pussy drip with anticipation.

"Don't make me wait any longer!" I gasped.

"Evie?"

Jeremy mounted himself above me, lining himself up with my opening. My breath came in short gasps as he slowly pushed down into me.

Yes... yes... YES!

"Evie!"

Something touched my shoulder. Something that felt like a hand. And it didn't feel like Jeremy's. In fact...

I didn't feel Jeremy at all anymore.

I suddenly sat up. Jeremy was supposed to be on top of me, giving me the long overdue fucking I had been craving. He wasn't. And the ground beneath me felt wrong. It wasn't soft dirt I felt beneath me, but hard basement floor. There was no open night sky above me; there was a ceiling. I was surrounded not by trees but instead by four bare walls.

"No... NO!" I screamed, suddenly jumping up and running to the wall, unable to accept that it was there. But it was there, perfectly solid under my hands, which began frantically clawing at it.

"I WAS OUT! I WAS OUT!"

"Evie! Hey!"

A hand fell on my shoulder again, and I turned to its source. I blinked at the sight of another face I felt like I had not seen in eons. "Charlene?"

"Your dad finally agreed to let me come down to visit you. I thought you'd want some company... unless you've got some already, so to speak?"

In spite of the things she'd said to me the last few times I'd seen her, I really was happy she was here...

Or was she?

After what I had just experienced, I couldn't be sure of anything now. I couldn't trust what I saw.

My brief smile vanished, and I scurried away from the apparition of Charlene, ducking into the corner. "No!" I whimpered, my hands grabbing my head. "You're not here! You're not real! You're in my head!"

"Evie! Come on, it's all right! I'm here!"

Breathing hard, I started to chant, "I'm losing my mind! I'm losing my mind! I'm losing my mind! I'm losing my mind!"

"Hey! Calm down! I'm really here!" Charlene exclaimed, dropping to her knees and pulling me into her arms, hugging my head to her chest and stroking my hair. "You're okay! You're okay! I'm here!"

As she held me I started to calm down, slowly beginning to consider the idea that she was really there. The fact that she was touching me lent some credence to her presence… but then, I had imagined Jeremy touching me too.

But something about this felt more genuine than any fantasy. The way her hands were tenderly stroking my head… there was nothing imagined about that.

I slowly lifted my head to her face. "Charlene?" I cautiously whispered.

She chuckled softly. "Yeah. Still me."

I finally let go. I threw my arms around her midsection and broke down crying against her belly.

CHAPTER ELEVEN

Eventually I regained my composure, and was able to start asking her questions. "How is everyone?"

"It's been weird out there," Charlene said. "It seems like everyone is either talking about you or the Morgandorfs. Half the pack has been saying how much they hate you and how they can't believe you betrayed us like you did. Others are saying how sad they are for you, either because of what your dad's doing, or because of how the Morgandorfs obviously brainwashed you."

"What do you say?"

Charlene paused, looking uncomfortable. "I wanted to hate you for a while, Evie. I'm not gonna lie. I know I said some things to you that… must've hurt."

"A little," I lied.

"But then that thing with your mom happened. She's still outside, chained to that stake. That was when a lot of us started thinking Leon was taking this too far, and we started pleading with Leon to make your dad let you out of here. And Leon would always just say that you weren't going anywhere until you'd renounced all ties to the Morgandorfs and all that."

"Yeah, I've heard it enough times from my dad."

"Well, the good thing about your mom being leashed outside is that anyone who wants to can walk right up and talk to her. So that's what I've been doing."

I frowned. "Then you can tell her I'm sorry about this. She's in that position because of me. I never meant to get her—"

"Hey, don't worry, it's okay! She doesn't blame you for anything! In fact, if anything, she's more on your side than ever now after this. She says all she did was open the door for you for a minute, and you didn't even get very far out of it, and if this is how Leon responds to that, well, she can understand that much more why you'd prefer anyone over him, even a Morgandorf."

In spite of myself, I choked out a chuckle and rolled my eyes.

Charlene paused for a moment, looking like she was contemplating hard what she was about to say next. "And, if you ask me, I'm starting to get the sense of why you'd go with that particular one, now that I've had the chance to talk to him a bit more."

I looked up at her, blinking in confusion. "Wait, what? What are you talking about?"

"Yeah…" she said, biting her lip. "I didn't think it was a good idea to tell anyone but you about this. Well, you and your mom."

"What is it?"

Charlene took a breath. "A couple days ago, I was out wandering the woods along the border, and I ran into him, just hanging around. So, naturally, the first thing I tried to do was chase him away. But he wouldn't budge, even when I threatened to rip out his entrails. He just kept asking about you. I kept on threatening him and telling him to get lost and everything, and he kept on trying to find out where you were, why he hadn't seen you, and all that. And finally I told him that you were locked up down here because of him." She paused again, getting a faraway look in her eye. "And then, like… the way he looked at me… and then the next thing he said, that really stuck with me. He said, 'That's what the pack that claims to love her does to her for choosing to love someone?' …And I just stood there, not sure what to say. I couldn't really think of anything to defend what we're doing to you after he said that."

I listened raptly, not saying anything yet.

"So, anyway, after that, I came to your mom, and I decided to tell her about it. I mean, I knew it was risky, 'cause if anyone else found out about it, I'd be in almost as much trouble as you. But I figured your mom didn't have any reason to rat on me. And it turned out she encouraged me to go back and meet him again, to see if I could come to understand him better. And, you know, I was hesitant. He was still a Morgandorf, you know. But I went. I ran into him again in the same place." She paused again, and added, "And he wasn't alone this time."

I leaned forward. "Who?"

"It was this girl… the Morgandorf alpha's daughter."

I couldn't help smiling when I heard that. "Andrea!" She was still there for me, trying to be my friend even now. That meant a lot.

"She told me I wasn't the only one who was going against her pack. She said if her father found out she was there, he would—and I quote—'rip out her insides, stuff her with goodies and string her up to use as a piñata.'"

I managed a small laugh. "Yeah, that's an Andrea line if I ever heard one."

"So, anyway, we got to talking, mostly about you. And before I knew it we were beginning to talk about a plan."

My eyebrows went up. "What kind of plan?"

At that point, Charlene turned to look up the stairs behind her, as if checking to see if anyone was listening. And then she stepped up to where I sat on the floor, and knelt down in front of me, leaning close to me to whisper, "We're working on a plan to get you out of here."

Well, I sure as hell perked up when I heard that. "How?"

"Shhh!" she said, putting a finger to her lips. "I've been going back and forth between Jeremy and your mom with this, discussing ideas and all that. We don't have all the details worked out yet. We're still working on it. But it's gonna involve creating some kind of big diversion, to get everyone somewhere else, on the other side of the village or maybe even out of it. And… here's the part you're not gonna like."

I grimaced. "What is it?"

"It's gonna have to wait at least another three days, when Leon lets your mom off of that chain."

I groaned, letting my head droop.

Charlene took hold of me by the shoulders. "Your dad is okay with me coming down to visit you," she said. "I'll be able to come keep you company from time to time, if that helps you keep your sanity. And we'll be working on bringing the plan together in the meantime. Trust me, we're gonna get you out of here."

That was enough for me, I decided. I lunged forward and threw my arms around her.

*

We spent the next few days in planning mode. As she said, Dad allowed Charlene to visit me whenever she wanted. I'm sure he'd have been a lot less generous if he'd cared to listen in on what we were talking about.

Through Charlene, I was kept apprised of what was going on outside that basement. There was a lot of talk among the pack about how they were going to make the Morgandorfs pay for how they'd "corrupted" me. Some of the pack wanted to respond in kind, by abducting one of theirs. Some suggested they should find Jeremy, saying that the party that picked me up should have gotten him too, lamenting all the lost time they could have been torturing him. Others wanted to simply wage a war of attrition, and make them all pay. Of course, most of these were the ones who had spent years looking for any excuse they could think of to march into Morgandorf territory and just kill them all outright.

I was gladdened to learn that not everyone was down with what Leon and my dad were doing. There were especially a lot who disapproved of Leon's treatment of my mom for what little she did for me. And even some of the ones who thought of me as a traitor felt that my punishment was being taken way too far. Some. Not enough to rally against Leon, though.

We were having a difficult time coming up with a plan that we felt comfortable using, because most of the ideas being tossed around usually opened the door for someone to get hurt. One advantage we had was that Andrea was still on our side, and since she hadn't been banished from the village the way Jeremy had, that meant if we needed to we could get her to stir up the Morgandorfs for something. Unfortunately, we couldn't seem to come up with a way to use that that didn't involve one pack attacking the other.

Still, even if our planning sessions weren't really going anywhere, I was more than grateful for Charlene's company. It meant the world to me that she didn't hate me anymore, and with her coming down to see me, I was able to sleep much better and keep from feeling like I was losing my mind.

And then came a day when Charlene came down those steps—and not alone.

There was Mom, coming down right behind her.

At once I bolted up from the corner I sat in and dashed into her open arms. "I'm so glad you're here!" I sobbed.

Mom pressed her face against mine and stroked along my spine. "I am too. I was so sad for my baby pup."

"They chained you up like a dog!" I whined. "Just for being good to me!"

"It doesn't matter what they do to me, Evie," Mom said. "Because I'm never going to stop caring about you."

Charlene let us hug it out for a while longer, before she finally had to step in. "Okay, as touching as this is, there is a reason we came down here."

I looked to her, seeing the determined expression on her face, and I started to get the idea. "You've got a plan?"

Mom and Charlene exchanged serious looks. "Yes, we do have something in mind," Mom said. "But I don't think you're going to like what it is."

I frowned. "What is it?" I deadpanned.

Charlene sighed. "Well… like you said, you didn't like any of the plans we came up with because they all involved someone attacking someone else.

And you wanted us to come up with a plan that didn't. Well…"

"Well what?"

Charlene swallowed uncomfortably. "We couldn't come up with one. So we came up with the best plan we could, and we're going with it."

"Hey, no! Don't do that! I don't want anyone getting hurt on my account!"

"It's our choice," Charlene said. "If we can help it, the only ones getting hurt will be us."

I didn't like the sound of that. "What is this plan exactly?"

Charlene looked to the floor, making an uncomfortable noise before answering. This couldn't be good.

"Oh, god, I'm gonna hate this plan, aren't I?"

Mom was the one who finally spoke up. "Charlene is going to convince the pack that she found your boyfriend, Jeremy. And she's going to tell them he attacked her. Then she's going to get them riled up to go find him and bring him back here, but she'll lead them in the wrong direction. Now for the ones who stay behind in the village, Andrea will tell the Morgandorfs that we attacked her and lead them here. When the rest of the pack tries to fight them off, I'll step in and try to mediate things. And while everyone's distracted, Jeremy will come in here and smuggle you out."

I looked back and forth at both of them like they were completely insane. Which for a moment, I honestly entertained the notion that they might be. "You're serious," I said, blinking at them. It was an observation, not a question.

"Completely," Charlene said.

"You don't think this is just begging to go completely wrong?" I shrugged.

"We know it's not a perfect plan," Mom said. "But it's the best we've been able to come up with."

"Well that doesn't speak very highly of the other options, because that's a terrible plan!"

"Yeah, we know," Charlene sighed. "And it gets worse."

My eyes widened, my brow furrowing. "Worse?"

Charlene cringed. "This is the part you're really not gonna like. We made the decision that to really get the pack riled up, we're going to have to make it look like Jeremy really attacked me. Bad."

"You mean…" I frowned, getting the picture and wishing I wasn't. "He's gonna… you can't do that for me!"

"It was my decision," Charlene said. And then she took a breath, letting me know she was about to say something else that I wouldn't like. "Just like it was Andrea's decision to have me do the same to her."

I grabbed my head. "Oh, god, this is going too far!"

Mom stepped forward, taking hold of my shoulders. "It's what everyone is willing to do to get you out of this!"

"But there's a million things that can go wrong here!" I protested. "If you bring the Morgandorfs here, who's to say you can stop them from hurting anyone else? And Charlene, what are you gonna do when the pack realizes you're leading them on a wild goose chase?"

"We know there's a lot of risk involved," Charlene said. "It's impossible to completely predict how everyone's going to react. So we can only plan things to a certain point and then play it by ear."

My head heavy, I stepped backward into the wall and sat down on the floor. "Oh, this is so messed up! This is so not what I wanted!"

"And having you locked up down here is not what we wanted," Mom said, stepping up and kneeling down in front of me. "You went to extreme measures for what you wanted. What we're doing is no different."

"It *is* different!" I protested. "What I did, I risked myself for no one *but* myself! You're all risking yourselves for me!"

"And that's our choice to make," Mom said. "We're doing it because we love you! You can't ask us to sit by idly while you waste away down here!"

I frowned, and looked away from her. Mom reached out to touch my face, bringing me back to face her. "I want you to understand something else,

Evelyn," she said. "I still don't completely trust that Morgandorf boy. Maybe that's my own prejudice as a Caldour talking, but that's how it is. So when I tell you I'm putting my safety on the line and putting yours in his hands, I want you to realize what a leap of faith I'm taking."

I regarded Mom hard. I did not like what they were planning to do… but as of this point, it was the only possibility I had heard for getting me out of that basement. And as long as I couldn't come up with a better option, I had no grounds to refuse them.

They stayed with me for another hour or two. It was the least they could offer. They finally left when Dad came down with my food, and suggested that they should leave now, reminding them that I was down here for a "reason." So then they left, casting me knowing looks as they walked up the stairs.

Then the door shut behind them, and I had nothing to do but wait.

*

Waiting sucked.

That's all there was to it. I was glad that there was a plan in place to get me out of there, but I couldn't stand that there was nothing I could do to contribute to it. Down there I was completely cut off, with no way of knowing how things were going. I didn't know if the plan had been put into motion yet, or how far along it might be, or if anything was going wrong. And of course, as I had pointed out, there was no end to things that could go wrong.

Hell, I wouldn't know anything until that door opened and Jeremy came in to whisk me away, by which point the plan would already have been completed. Or until someone else came in, like Dad or Leon. At which point I could probably assume it had all gone to hell in a hand basket.

I ended up spending several long hours doing nothing but nervously pacing. All the things I didn't know were driving me out of my mind. Had Charlene already forced Jeremy to "attack" her? Had she already done the same to Andrea? Were the Morgandorfs on the way? Would Mom be able to stop them when they got here? What if the hunting party picked up Jeremy's actual scent trail, and followed him back here? Or what if they realized Charlene was leading them the wrong way and turned on her?

God dammit, I'd have given anything to be able to know what was happening outside!

The only thing that had a chance of telling me anything was that little window, which only afforded me a slight view of the village from an odd angle. It was still hard to make out anything that was going on in the village from it, which was all the more frustrating now.

But thankfully, I was soon given a little bit of insight. As I stood on my tiptoes to look out that window, straining to see anything interesting, a pair of feet stepped up to the window. The figure knelt down, revealing my mom's face. She looked around, checking for any witnesses, and bent forward.

"We're ready," she said. "Charlene is on her way back to the village now to show off her wounds, and Andrea is on her way back to the Morgandorf village. Just sit tight."

Then she walked away. I relaxed my stance, dropping my heels back to the floor. Okay, that was helpful at least. A little. But there was still plenty of room for everything to go wrong.

And once again, I was back to waiting.

I'm sure I was only waiting a short while after that; maybe ten minutes at the most. It felt like a lot longer, though. But I heard a howl off in the distance, and peeking out the window, I could make out the indications of some kind of commotion going on. Many members of the pack were crowding around what presumably must have been Charlene, and while I couldn't make out what anyone was saying from where I was, I could tell there were a lot of loud words being exchanged. Some of them particularly loud.

There was discussion and argument, which from where I stood, unable to hear them, seemed to take forever. But after an agonizingly long wait, I could see a large group of them branching away, shifting into their four-legged forms as they headed off into the woods.

Okay then. It looked like that much had worked. So far, so good. Fingers crossed.

So then I waited some more. I went back to pacing, wishing I could be out there, seeing what was happening, or helping to make it happen. But of course, if I'd been out there we wouldn't have been doing this in the first place, so wishing for that was pointless.

A while later, I heard some more howls, the kind meant to be used as a battle cry. It sounded like the Morgandorfs had arrived. But this time I couldn't see anything from the angle of my little window. But there were some loud voices carrying through the village; from where I was, I could make out that much.

I went and stood near the bottom of the stairs. If the Morgandorfs were here, and if everything had gone right, then Jeremy should be coming through that door any minute.

Any minute…

Any minute…

Come on, door, open!

Seconds ticked by. Then a minute. Then another. The door remained shut. Every muscle in my body held tense, ready to spring forward the second someone came through it… the very second…

Finally I did hear someone moving up there. I allowed myself to become excited; Jeremy was coming. I was finally getting out of here! I was finally going to be free!

I heard footsteps coming up to the door. I heard the latch unlocking.

The knob turned.

The door swung open.

And I staggered back, falling backward onto the floor as Dad came marching down the steps.

"Dad!" I gasped. "What are... why are you...?"

"Expecting someone else, Evelyn?" Dad probed.

That shut me up quickly.

Dad ducked down and snatched me up by the wrist, pulling me up to face him. "Do you know what's going on here?"

"Dad, please... you're hurting me!"

"Do you know why an attack party of your precious Morgandorfs is in the village, demanding blood? Or why your mother is out there now, trying to stop us from driving them out?"

"Dad..."

He pulled me right up to his face, which began to shift slightly, his eyes turning yellow and his teeth growing long and pointed, with some fur growing from his face. *"What did you do?"* he growled.

I had seen my dad's fury before. I had definitely been on the receiving end of it enough times. But I had never seen it rear its head like this. I honestly couldn't answer him, purely because I was too terrified of him to say anything.

But then we heard another growl. Turning around behind him, another wolf was poised with tail up and fur bristling, showing his teeth from the top of those stairs.

Even if I hadn't recognized him by sight even in his lupine form, his scent would have identified him for me immediately. Jeremy had come for me, just like we planned. It was just our bad luck that someone else was here first.

Dad whirled around, throwing me behind him. "Get out of my house, Morgandorf scum!"

Undaunted, Jeremy advanced down the stairs, continuing his threatening growls. I jumped forward, grabbing onto my dad's arm and looking around his shoulder. "Jeremy, please don't hurt him! He's still my dad!"

But apparently, Dad wasn't going to brook my involvement. His arm snapped out and shoved me roughly back down to the floor, where I landed with a grunt. When I looked up, Dad was quickly stripping his clothes off as he started to shift. The next moment, two angry and ferocious wolves faced each other, baring their fangs and trading fierce growls.

If the two of them came down to it, one of them was likely to kill the other. If that happened… not only would I lose one, but I'd never be able to look at the other the same way again.

No. I couldn't let this happen. I couldn't allow anyone I loved to die on my account, least of all at the hands of someone else I loved.

I sprang up onto all fours as I shifted to my lupine shape, and forward I charged, barreling into my dad and shoving him out of Jeremy's way. Dad lifted his head from where he'd tumbled to the floor, and stared at me with his wolf's eyes in disbelief. I only spared a momentary glance down at him, before I turned my gaze to Jeremy, and nodded to the open door behind him. Our way out was there, and I wanted to waste no more time down here.

Apparently, neither did he.

Both of us turned and started bolting up the stairs for that door—to which I made it all of two strides before I felt Dad's jaws close around my right hind leg, yanking me back and dropping me flat down on the stairs. Looking behind me, Dad was pulling down at my leg, desperately trying to keep me down here in his personal dungeon, his eyes turned up to me with a burning determination.

Jeremy's fur-covered shape went flying over my head, pouncing on Dad and pinning him down, forcing him to release me. I took only a moment to nurse my leg; the wound wasn't that deep anyway.

I was much more concerned about what was happening below. The fight that I had just tried to prevent was breaking out right in front of me. Trying to get them apart from each other before they came to blows was one thing, but now that they were actually rearing up on their hind legs, fighting tooth and claw, there was little I could think to do to pull them apart.

Other than to take a side.

So I rushed in beside Jeremy, rearing back on my hind legs and clawing at my father, baring my teeth to him. Once that happened, Dad suddenly had much less will to fight. The fact that his daughter was actually fighting him, physically, was a bit too much to deal with. Jeremy and I stood there, staring him down, and all he could do was bristle.

This time, when Jeremy nodded back to the door, and we again made a break for it, Dad didn't stop me.

CHAPTER TWELVE

I didn't spare a glance back at the house, or at the confrontation happening out in the village. All my attention was focused on the forest ahead of me. All I could see were those trees, and the freedom they offered.

Within seconds, the open world around me had given way to the shade of trees and foliage. After all that time in that basement, it was like diving into a swimming pool after weeks in the desert. And still I continued to run. The village was always too close behind me; I wanted—no, needed—to put it as far from me as I could. That place had become my prison, and as far as I was concerned at that moment, I wouldn't have shed a tear if I never saw it again.

So we just ran, until we couldn't run anymore. We stopped in the middle of a clearing, no longer with any idea of where we were in relation to either village. We paused a moment to catch our breath— and then I looked up to Jeremy. Simultaneously, we shifted to our two-legged forms.

And then we *launched* ourselves at each other.

A part of me kept expecting to wake up from this. I thought at any moment all this would crumble away, and I would be back in that basement again. But as my tongue probed Jeremy's mouth and my hands roamed all over his body, every sense I had told me that this was all completely real. He was really here. I really had him again.

"Don't ever go away from me again!" I pleaded with him between kisses.

"I was going to say the same to you," he said. "All those days I spent hovering around the village, just hoping I might catch a glimpse of you, not knowing where you were or what they were doing to you…"

"You think you had it bad?" I said. "I damn near lost my fucking mind in that basement! I mean, can you imagine, being locked down there with barely any sunlight, surrounded by nothing but four walls, with only a bucket to go in? I couldn't even keep track of time in there, let alone reality!"

"Here's reality now, Evie," Jeremy smirked as he grabbed a handful of my ass and yanked me against his crotch. I yelped and giggled, and kissed him deeply.

After that, I turned and slowly slipped out of his grasp, staring up at the sky with a big smile, holding out my arms and twirling around. "Sky!" I cheered "I can actually see the sky! I never thought I'd miss the sky!" I inhaled a deep breath through my nose, savoring the good, clean forest air, after spending so long with the only air I had to breathe being stale and suffocating. I twirled around some more, collapsing down in the dirt, and sighing contentedly, wanting to roll around in that dirt, perhaps even to take a bath in it. "Soft ground!" I hummed loudly. "I never knew how much I loved dirt! I want to sleep in this dirt every night! Forever and ever!"

Jeremy smiled, and knelt down over me. "How do you feel about doing it in this dirt every night?"

I grinned from ear to ear. "That's pretty good too."

My hand came up to stroke the side of his face, still delighted by the mere feel of his flesh under my fingers. He bent down, bringing his lips down to mine, and my arms arose to wrap around his neck. After all the days I had spent dreaming of this moment, all the nights I had lied awake wishing he were with me again, everything I had longed for was finally here. I had him in my arms, his kiss on my lips. And for once, I knew this was no fantasy.

Especially after someone else came along to confirm it.

"Whoa! Okay! I know I just saw something I'm too young for!"

I lifted my head to see Andrea standing among the trees a few feet from us, dressed in shorts and a tank and shielding her eyes. "Andrea!" I beamed, pushing Jeremy off and scrambling to my feet so I could rush forward and embrace her.

"Ow!" she gasped as soon as I grabbed her.

I instantly recoiled, suddenly remembering the part of the plan I'd never particularly approved of. "Oh, god, I'm sorry!" I said. "Are you okay?"

Andrea turned and lifted her shirt, showing me the bandage on her back along her side, just below her arm. "Charlene has one hell of a bite," she said. "But I'll recover. I agreed to it, anyway."

I immediately felt terrible for her. "I'm so sorry about this," I said. "I told Charlene and my mom I didn't like this plan! I never wanted anyone else to suffer for me!"

"But you're out of there, aren't you?" she said. "And all I had to do for it was endure a little bite."

"Which you just called one hell of a bite," I reminded.

"The point is, compared to what you've been through, I think this is a fair price, don't you?"

"How did it go with the pack?" Jeremy asked her.

Andrea shrugged. "About like we expected. Tell the truth, it was kind of scary how easy it was to get them riled up. All I did was show them the bite once and they were practically howling for blood. Literally. I thought they were gonna trample Ricardo to death when he tried to get them to calm down and think this out. But we got the kind of attack party we were going for without too much trouble."

"How did you find us here?" I asked her. "I kind of thought we were running pretty aimlessly… in fact, I don't even know where we are now."

"I followed your scent from your village," she shrugged.

"So you did go along with the attack party?" Jeremy asked. "I thought we agreed that was a dangerous idea?"

"Oh, I didn't go along with them. Exactly. I mean my dad wouldn't let me go with them anyway. So I just snuck away after them once they got me bandaged up. I went as fast as I could walk on two legs—which, I gotta say, I never knew how much traveling on only two legs sucks. But I can't shift form without tearing my bandage off. But I got to the Caldour village just in time to find the two of you sneaking away, so I just kind of snuck after you. Which, again, would've been a lot easier if I could've shifted form. That's the worst part about this whole deal," she continued, lifting her shirt again to look down her back at her bandage. "For the next few days I'm stuck with two legs. But I guess after what you've been through I can't complain."

"Wait," I said. "If you saw us, and you could follow us, couldn't somebody else?"

"I don't think so," Andrea said, turning her eyes up in thought. "I was the only one looking for you. Everyone else was too busy yelling at each other.

"Her father will be looking for us," Jeremy pointed out. "If you could track us, you can be damn sure he will."

I frowned. Jeremy was absolutely right. "We've gotta keep moving," I said. "Find a stream somewhere we can lose our scent trails."

"I think I know where to find one," Andrea said. "This way."

We followed her for a short distance, clambering over logs and brush, before coming to a trickling stream where Jeremy and I ducked and began washing ourselves. We then waded upstream, letting it carry our scents away, getting a good distance from where we'd gone in before we stepped out and wandered aimlessly away.

Once I was confident that no one who was looking for us would be able to track us, we relaxed against the base of a tree, where I curled up against Jeremy once more. "Can you find your way back home from here?" Jeremy asked Andrea.

Andrea scoffed. "Please. These woods are my playground. I could find my way back with a bag over my head!"

"Glad to hear it," I deadpanned. "You should get back there before you're too badly missed."

She nodded, becoming more serious. "I'll make my appearance. But as soon as it's clear, I should meet up with Charlene to touch base. You two should lay low in the meantime."

I nodded. "Yeah. We'll wait here for you."

"Maybe we shouldn't stay in one place," Jeremy suggested. "Last time we tried that, we woke up to find someone dragging you away."

"Okay," Andrea said, turning her head down in thought. "What about… that little grove south of the Morgandorf village. Remember the one, Evelyn? We used to sneak away there to gossip in private."

"I remember it," I said. "But don't the Morgandorfs know about that place?"

"The Morgandorfs aren't looking for us," Jeremy pointed out. "It's only the Caldours we're worried about right now, and even if they did manage to track us there, I doubt they'd want to come that close to the Morgandorf village unless they were looking for trouble."

"Knowing my dad, I don't think that would stop him," I muttered.

"You go ahead back," Jeremy said to Andrea. "We'll find our way there. Later."

Andrea's mouth turned up in a smirk. "Yeah. I'm guessing there's only so much longer you guys can keep it PG-13."

Damn. The kid needed to stop talking; she was giving me ideas!

She started heading off then. "I'll give you two your privacy now. I'll catch you later."

As she scurried away into the brush, I turned my attention to Jeremy, who was sporting a pretty heavy look, aimed off into the distance. "What are you thinking?" I asked.

"I'm thinking, we got you out of there, you're finally free, and we can do what we want and go where we want again. But I'm just wondering what that'll be. Do we run away like we were talking about before? Do we keep trying to make peace? Do we dare take any kind of chance that they might catch us again? And even if we do run, who's to say we'll ever be safe?"

I climbed onto his lap, taking hold of his face. "Hey. We can worry about that later. We're here now. We're together."

"We let our guard down before," he said. "Look what happened."

I yanked his face to look me in the eye. "Jeremy, listen. I'm free. I finally have you again. I don't want to think about our problems right now, not after I spent over a week with nothing to do but think about them. So can we please just worry about this later?"

"Evelyn, if we get complacent—"

"Jeremy, please! Just shut up and fuck me!"

When I pulled him to my waiting lips, he stopped trying to fight me. My tongue reached for his, finding it not quite matching the hunger mine had. At least, not at first. After a minute or two, he started to get with it, and I started to feel how much he had missed me.

And he had missed me. A *lot*.

His arms engulfed me, trapping me in his constricting grasp. Even if I wanted to, I would be going nowhere. I gasped as he began kissing my neck, pressing my chest against him as my fingers stirred about through his hair. With my crotch grinding against his lap, it didn't take long before I started to feel him swelling to full hardness, his shaft rising up to press into my mound.

I very slowly began to lean backward as he took my tits into his mouth. His head rotated about, his tongue making lazy patterns around my nipple, making me moan loudly. God, I had missed this. So many times in that basement I had dreamed about being back with him, feeling him pleasuring me like this. Sometimes I had even let myself believe I really was with him again, imagining it almost as vividly as if it were really happening. But nothing could ever compare to what I was feeling now. No fantasy could come close to replacing Jeremy's actual lips on my breast.

Or, for that matter, his lips on my clit, once he finally laid me down on my back and got his head between my legs. He slowly lowered me down, bathing my belly in his kisses, until I was flat on my back, squirming on the ground and clawing at dirt and leaves around me as he expertly tongued my sopping pussy.

When he brought me to orgasm, it was like suddenly tasting a favorite meal again after a yearlong fast. I honestly couldn't believe how much I needed that. He paused in his ministrations after I stopped screaming and thrashing, and I just lay there panting for a moment, staring up at the sky—that beautiful blue sky, not a ceiling, see through that rustling canopy of vibrant green leaves bathed in golden sunlight…

Life was truly wonderful!

I determined to make life wonderful for Jeremy too, by sitting up and taking hold of his cock, giving it a few strokes before I ducked my head and took him into my mouth. Good god, I even missed this! I never knew how much I loved sucking Jeremy's cock until I'd been denied it for so long! I found myself involuntarily moaning happily around that big thing filling my mouth, running my tongue languidly around the spongy crown, savoring it as if it were a favorite treat. And for all intents and purposes, it was.

He lifted my head to look up at him, and then lowered me back down again as he knelt above me, positioning himself between my legs. My whole body quivered, panting with arousal. "Put it in me!" I pleaded. "Please! I need it now!"

Thankfully, he didn't keep me waiting another second. The feeling of his cockhead parting my wet lips, pushing into me and steadily sliding inside was the greatest relief I could have imagined. At that moment, I wasn't sure exactly how I'd managed to not kill myself in that basement, being forced to go without this for so long. I felt like I wanted to live the rest of my life with him inside of me. Why did I never know until now just how unbelievably wonderful sex with Jeremy was—and we'd barely gotten started!

I reached my hands up to wrap around his shoulders as he leaned down over me, meeting my eyes with his own. Those big, beautiful eyes of his. My hands stroked along the muscles of his arms, feeling the curves of his biceps, and then went up again to feel the tones of his back… there was literally nothing about him that I wasn't in love with.

He thrust into me deeply, eliciting a loud grunt from me. He lowered himself atop me, letting me wrap my arms around him fully, digging my fingers into his back. I started moaning loudly as he built up a rhythm, fucking me slow and steady, nestling his face into the crook of my neck. My legs came up along his sides, hooking themselves over his thighs.

I had always loved being fucked by Jeremy. That much was certain. He'd always been the best I'd ever had. I had never had any illusions otherwise.

But this… it almost felt like the first time. I could swear, in all the times we'd been together, sex with him had never been this good. I was practically coming already. Maybe it was because I was just that excited about finally being with him again after I'd spent all that time not sure if I ever would, but it really didn't matter. All that was important was that I had him.

And good god, did he have me.

I grabbed him by the hair and yanked his head up so that I could start raining frantic little kisses all over his face. I honestly had never felt this strongly for anyone before. I got excited enough that I aggressively lunged upward, and ended up rolling us over, while I continued bathing his face in my kisses. "I love you," I whispered in between rapid-fire kisses. "I love you. I love you." I continued to repeat that again and again. "I love you so much, Jeremy."

He didn't answer verbally, at least not at first. He finally took hold of my face in his hands, holding me steady and stopping my rain of kisses. And then he just looked at me. And even without him saying it, I could see him thinking the same thing. It was all over his face. It was clearly written in his eyes.

And it was definitely spelled out in his kiss, when he brought my head down to his lips.

I sat upright and started to grind my hips on his lap. I could gaze down at his face, and see his expression of love staring back up at me, while my hands could feel up those wonderful, rock-hard pectorals of his. His strong hands held me by my hips, and slid up and down my sides, feeling up the shape of my figure like a clay sculptor working with his pottery on a turntable. I took hold of his wrists and brought his hands up to grasp my bouncing breasts, and rolled my head back with a moan when he palmed my nipples and began to knead the flesh of my tits.

Jeremy sat up, his hands pressing onto my back as he kissed me deeply, and my arms wrapped around his neck to accept him while my hips continued to move on his lap. We remained like that for a while, sitting up together while making out and steadily fucking, both sets of my lips securely fastened to him.

We only broke that position when he grew too tired to continue sitting up. So in order to keep my mouth attached to his, I had to follow him down, now laying atop him again, my breasts rubbing back and forth on his chest with my humping motions.

He eventually rolled us over again, seeming now like he was trying to devour my whole mouth as he thrust down into me. I found myself caught between being driven to roll my head back to let out a pleasured moan, and yet not wanting to disengage from his lips. So I was left to fill his mouth with the sounds of my pleasure.

I don't know how long we continued to roll around in the dirt like that. We must have switched between who was on top at least a dozen times. And I think I came almost as many times. But what I did know for sure was that if I'd had my way about it, we never would have stopped.

But all the same, the climax I had right around the time he finally fired off inside was worth having to let it end. I suppose.

Trying to catch my breath while his weight was lying on top of me probably wasn't the brightest idea, but I wouldn't have traded the feeling for anything. For a long while, the only sound to be heard, apart from the chirping of birds and the rustling of leaves around us, was the sound of our heavy breathing.

The silence was finally broken by Jeremy softly saying, "You know, we are trying to avoid being found. You probably alerted everyone around for miles where we are with the way you screamed."

I blushed, putting my hands up to my face as I started to laugh. He probably had a point, in all seriousness; there was a good chance that anyone who might have been looking for us might have heard us after all that. But still, the way he said it was just funny. In a humiliating but also endearing sort of way.

"Seriously, we should probably get moving before someone finds us," he grunted, as he finally started to peel himself away from my sweaty body.

"Okay," I sighed. "But let's not tire ourselves out too much getting wherever we go."

"Why not?" he asked.

I replied with a raised eyebrow and a mischievous smirk. "'Cause you're gonna need more energy for what I'm gonna do to you later, big guy!"

*

I know I'm continuing to beat a dead horse about this point, but there's really nothing like an extended confinement to make you appreciate the things you usually take for granted. Especially the things that have always made you feel the freest.

When we shifted to our four-legged forms and ran off into the forest, it was like I had almost forgotten what running felt like. Yes, we'd run when we escaped from the Caldour village, but that was just to get away. There wasn't time then to really appreciate it.

But I sure as hell appreciated it this time. The feel of the wind rushing through my fur, the ground beneath my paws, the world flying by me as I propelled myself forward...

This was what I lived for.

I mean, besides the wolf running beside me. He was the other thing I lived for.

The wind soon brought the scent of a deer to our noses. We immediately changed direction, moving to catch our newly discovered prey. We weaved through trees and brush, catching sight of the docile herbivore moments before it sensed our approach. We were within five feet of it when it finally broke out into a run, racing to escape us. So we had a chase given to us and we responded like the wolves we were.

Rock, tree, rose bush, whatever it may have been that barred our path was paid no mind. We pursued our quarry with single-minded determination. Nothing else mattered but our pursuit.

And like a two-pronged instrument of death, we closed in on the animal, Jeremy leaping at it from the right, catching its throat in his jaws, while I lunged forward from the left, biting into its side. It came down hard, as we stood triumphant over it, and Jeremy squeezed with his jaws on its neck once more, choking the last bit of life from our prey.

For the first time in however long I had been locked away, I ate with pride. I feasted happily on our kill, relishing in the feel of living like a wolf again, instead of like a prisoner. I recalled all the meals that Dad had brought me in that basement that I had simply ignored or pushed away, or even thrown at him. Or if I had eaten at all, it was usually with disinterest and lethargy. It was only when I'd gotten to the point of being so famished that I was ready to eat the house down—which, I kid not, was an idea that had crossed my mind a couple times while I was down there—that I really dug into the food that Dad would bring me.

So now, with the taste of fresh-killed meat in my mouth and the love of my life by my side, I felt like nothing in the world could go wrong again.

Of course, my head knew better, but I allowed myself this moment of elation. I'd had so few of them lately.

After we'd eaten our fill, we rested for a while, and then navigated the forest back to that grove we'd agreed on with Andrea. No one was there when we arrived, so we decided to just chill for a while. We shifted to our two-legged forms and curled up together under a tree.

"So is this what we're gonna call home for the foreseeable future?" Jeremy asked in a soft voice.

"I could get used to it," I said. "After living trapped in a basement, anyplace with open air and sky above me will do."

"Better hope it doesn't rain," he remarked.

I chuckled softly. "If it started raining right now, you know what I'd do?"

"Tell me."

"I'd get up and start dancing in it. Hell, I might even go all Gene Kelly and burst into song."

Now it was Jeremy's turn to laugh. "You know, I don't think I've ever heard you sing before."

"Well, you're not missing much."

"But if it started to rain you'd assail me with it? What crime could I have committed?"

I playfully smacked him on the chest, laughing merrily as I jumped up onto his chest. "You jerk hole!"

He laughed back, and then we kissed.

"Point is, I'd love a little rain," I said. "Feeling raindrops falling on my skin… right now, I think that'd be wonderful!"

"And once the pneumonia set in, what then?"

"Then you can carry me in your big strong arms to the big, beautiful house you've built for us with your own two hands, and nurse me back to health. Lots of mouth-to-mouth required, of course."

"Of course," he said—right before swatting me on the ass.

My mouth dropped open in a scandalized "O", even as I laughed.

We continued to banter for a while longer, and eventually dozed off under the tree, my head pillowed on his chest.

*

The next thing I remember was waking up slowly, finding the sky beginning to darken. And then finding the faces of Andrea and Charlene looking down at us with adoring little smiles on their faces.

I suddenly sat up, inadvertently waking Jeremy in the process. "Hey, uh… there you are… how long have you two been there?"

"About five minutes maybe," Charlene shrugged.

"Five minutes?" I gasped. "Why didn't you wake us?"

"How could we disturb you when you looked so happy there?" Andrea teased. "Besides, you guys are so cute together!"

"Great," Jeremy muttered. "Just what I was going for."

"So what's going on back home?" I asked.

"Well, your mother managed to keep everyone from ripping each other to pieces," Charlene said. "At least long enough to convince the Morgandorfs to leave before anyone got hurt. So that was a plus. But that was before the word got out that you were gone. Of course, most of the pack seems to be under some kind of impression that a Morgandorf kidnapped you from your dad's basement while they were all distracted. A lot of them were saying they should never have let the Morgandorfs walk away, and some of them want to go march over to their village to find out where they have you. Apparently, the idea that you might have voluntarily left is a bit too much for some of them to grasp."

"Well, my pack was a little more calm," Andrea said "At least as far as the Caldours were concerned. I had some explaining to do."

"About what?" Jeremy asked.

"About where *I* went," she moaned. "I got back right after everyone else did. So, yeah, they did kinda notice I was gone."

"How'd that go over?" I asked.

Andrea sighed. "Well, Dad got me with that whole 'answer me now, girly' stare that he does. You remember, you've seen him do that."

"You mean like that time you weren't at the howl because you were off making out with Pete in your dad's bedroom?"

Andrea grimaced. "Yeah. Like that. Anyway, he started grilling me, and I decided to give him at least part of the true story. I mean nothing about you or Jeremy or Charlene or anything, but I told him that I followed the attack party to the village. Which, you know, my dad considers enough to ground me for twenty years to life. But I couldn't come up with anything convincing to cover with."

"How did he take it?" Jeremy asked.

She frowned. "I'm confined to my room for the next three days. Which, technically means I'm breaking parole right now. You're lucky I'm a trained master of sneaking out."

"At least it looks like we're in the clear," I offered. "That's something." Then I took a look at Charlene, and saw the bandages on her, covering her upper arm and shoulder. I cringed. "Damn, Jeremy, that's what you did to her?"

"Like I said, my idea," Charlene said, reaching a hand to her shoulder. "Doesn't even hurt that bad anymore. Really, I'm okay. We all are." She looked around at us as she said this. "You know, can I just say something?"

I blinked, raising an eyebrow. "You've never needed my permission before," I said. "This should be interesting."

Charlene paused. "I was a bitch. To all of you. I was brought up to hate Morgandorfs. I never stopped to question it. And I let it come between you and me, Evie. When you found someone to love, I should have been happy for you, but I could never see past the Morgandorf label. So I said things to you that... I'm sorry. That's really all I can say. I'm sorry for what I said to you... and you, Jeremy. The things I called you because of where you came from... were wrong. There's so much I shouldn't have said. And I know nothing I've done now can make up for any of that..."

"That's where you're wrong," I said, rising to my feet and stepping toward her. "You've done more than I could've ever asked for. Literally, I didn't ask you to take a bite for me," I added, deadpan. "But you helped get me out of there, and got me back to Jeremy. No amount of words can diminish that."

Charlene smiled, and I saw a tiny little teardrop falling from her eye. I stepped forward and embraced her, and felt her embrace me back.

"What changed your mind?" Jeremy asked. "Am I that charming?" he added with a smirk.

Charlene chuckled a little. "No, actually, it wasn't you. It was her," she said, looking to Andrea.

"Me?"

"However charming Jeremy was, I could always still imagine the face of the conniving, deceitful Morgandorfs I'd always heard about hiding in him somewhere. I was always sure he had some ugly motive behind whatever he was doing, just because it was what I'd been told the Morgandorfs did. But Andrea... this bright-eyed Morgandorf pup who didn't have a hateful bone in her body... I could just tell that nothing I'd been told about your pack was true about her."

Andrea smiled, and stepped up to join us, forming a three-way hug. "Oh, okay, now this is happening," Charlene said.

I finally pulled away when Jeremy came up behind me, placing his hand on my shoulder. I backed into his arms, and let Charlene and Andrea continue embracing—although I could see Charlene starting to feel a bit awkward about it. But as she was learning, an object of Andrea's affections would not easily get away.

"Aww, isn't this touching," said a voice.

We all suddenly turned around to find an uninvited guest standing about ten feet away, looking at us with a cruel grin, surrounded by four wolves in their four-legged forms. We'd all been so worried about either Leon or my dad coming to find us here, none of us had stopped to worry about this one.

"Lucius!" I gasped. It didn't take much to identify the wolves flanking him as his backup party of Brock, Regan, Riley and Ennis.

"What are you doing here?" Andrea demanded.

"Funny, I was about to ask you the same question. Unless I'm completely fucktarded, I thought I heard your dad tell you you were grounded for running off when he told you not to. I kinda wanted to know where you were running to… and it looks like I found out."

Lucius began advancing on us, focused on Andrea. "Somebody's been a very, *very* bad girl!" he said, before grabbing her by the wrist, eliciting a shriek from her. "I think your daddy's gonna be interested to hear how you've been sneaking out to go palling around with Caldours! *Two* of them!"

"Let me go!" Andrea protested, struggling against him.

"You heard her!" Jeremy barked. "Get your hands off her!"

"You keep out of this, Caldour-lover!" Lucius snapped. "You're not part of this pack anymore, or did you forget that part?"

Charlene lunged forward, roughly shoving Lucius away from Andrea, while growing out her teeth and turning her eyes a lupine yellow. "Back off, shithead!" she growled.

Lucius's sly look turned one of rage, appalled at what had just happened. "No Caldour touches me and lives to talk about it!" he threatened. The wolves backing him up started to growl menacingly.

"You want a piece of me?" Charlene countered.

"Charlene, no!" I warned.

But Lucius made no reaction to me, focusing his fury on Charlene. "No," he said, his teeth growing out and his voice deepening. "I don't want a piece of you. I want lots of pieces!"

Andrea rushed in front of him, holding up her hands to stop him. "Lucius, don't!" But he only shoved her aside, pushing her down onto the ground to clear his path. He marched forward, lowering down to the ground as he shifted to his four-legged form.

Charlene seemed fully willing to back up her bravado, even against the wall of not one but five sets of teeth bearing down on her. And in fact she was already beginning to remove her clothes and trying to shift form. But as soon as her flesh and muscles started to change shape, the wound she had received from Jeremy to sell our story reasserted itself, and she stopped to grab her bandaged shoulder.

Given more time, I don't doubt she could have still fought through the pain and changed shape; I'd seen her shift form with a fresh wound plenty of times. But Lucius was rushing at her, and he was rushing fast.

There wasn't time for me to think about what I was doing. It all just happened in a flash. Before I knew what was happening, I had leapt forward, shifting form in mid-air, catching Lucius seconds before his teeth would have reached Charlene.

I didn't even realize I'd bitten into him until I tasted blood in my mouth.

And it wasn't until I was standing over him, with him lying on the ground looking up at me, that I realized I'd bitten into his throat.

I raised my head, blood dripping from my fangs, to look at Lucius's entourage, who had stopped dead in their tracks. Below my paws, Lucius was squirming, gasping for breath as blood pooled around his neck. When I looked at the wound I'd given him, I could see he was beyond any hope of recovery.

All I could do was finish him off.

In all my life, I had never killed another wolf before. I had never had any wish to. And I had no wish to now. But the heavy reality before me was inescapable; there was no backing out of this now.

So I brought my head down and clamped my teeth onto his throat again, making a sharp jerking motion to squeeze out his last breath.

When I looked up again, Lucius's followers were hurrying away, disappearing into the brush, making their way back to the Morgandorf village.

I sat back on my haunches, staring down at the bloody body of Lucius before me. Jeremy, Andrea and Charlene all stood around me, looking down at me wide-eyed in shock. "Evie…" Charlene breathed.

"What did you do?" Andrea quivered.

I slowly began backing away, shifting to my two-legged form and rising to my feet as I backed into Jeremy's arms. My hand came up to cover my mouth, which I found still wet, and I spit out the blood still on my lips. "I... I didn't want... I was just trying..."

"He would've killed us," Jeremy tried to reassure me. "You know that. You did what you had to do."

He was probably right. Lucius definitely had murder in his eyes. My case wasn't hard to argue here.

That didn't make me feel any less sick.

"Oh my god, they're gonna tell everyone in the pack what happened here! They're all gonna be looking for us now! They're gonna find us, and they're gonna... what are they gonna do?"

"Not all of us," I choked. "Just me. They're gonna be hunting me. *Everyone's* gonna be looking for me now!"

Jeremy breathed hard. "She's right. We can't stay here."

"Well, I can't go back!" Andrea cried, visibly panicking. "Not now! Not after this! They're gonna tell everyone I was here with you guys! They're gonna know I was here for this, and my dad... I can't even think about what he's gonna do to me!"

"No!" I said, rushing forward to take hold of her shoulders. "This isn't on you! Not for a second! This is all me! You didn't have anything to do with this! Your dad will understand that! I mean, he's your dad! What can he do to you?"

"Your dad locked you in a basement," she pointed out.

I couldn't argue with that.

"Andrea," Jeremy said, stepping toward her, "you're fourteen. You're too young to run away. You need a pack. And... regardless of what just happened here, you still have one. Ricardo won't send you away or do anything to hurt you. You're still his only daughter."

"It's bad enough they're gonna be hunting me for what I just did," I said. "We don't need him hunting you, too. And if you run away with us, Ricardo will move Heaven and Earth to find you."

Andrea looked all kinds of distressed. I could see her teenage mind struggling to grasp what to do. I knew because it was exactly how I felt.

"But they're gonna want to know where you are," Andrea said. "They're gonna want me to tell 'em!"

I nodded. She was absolutely right. "So you can't know," I said. "We have to disappear. We can't ever come back."

Those words felt like stones in my chest. This was never how I wanted things to go. I wanted to make peace between our packs. I wanted my family to be able to interact with Jeremy's without them trying to kill each other. I wanted to have a life with him that my friends and family could still be part of.

I could no longer see any hope of that. The only way for us to have any semblance of a life now was to sever all previous ties; to disappear into the woods and never look back.

Andrea looked on the verge of collapse. She suddenly came flying at me, enveloping me in her embrace as her tears started to fall freely. "Please don't make me go back there!" she cried. "If you go, I'll never see you again!"

"And if you go with us, you'll never see your family again," I said. "Is that what you want?"

Her lip quivered, but she shook her head.

"I'm sorry it happened this way," I said. "I'm gonna miss you so much!"

Andrea hugged me harder, wetting my belly with her tears.

Charlene came up behind her, putting a hand on her shoulder. "Come on, Andie," she said. "We should get back where we each belong."

Andrea let go of me briefly, before she latched onto Jeremy, hugging the hell out of him for a moment. And then she finally turned away, her face positively streaked with her tears. And then she let Charlene guide her away by the shoulder, looking back at us right up until she disappeared into the woods. Then I was left alone with Jeremy again. Him and the body of Lucius.

At which point I finally let go of the bile I'd been holding back. I dropped to my knees, doubled over and puked.

THE FINAL CHAPTER

Jeremy and I ran almost all night. We actively sought out every source of water we could swim across to lose our scent trails, finally coming to a stop around the crack of dawn up near the top of a cliff. We curled up together to get a few hours of sleep before we determined to set out again.

I think it was around midday when I woke up again, while Jeremy was still sleeping next to me. I didn't see fit to wake him yet; I sat up, looking off into the distance, seeing the expansive view over the nearby cliff. If I'd been on vacation, I might have been taken in by the beautiful view. As it was, all I could do was barely appreciate the miniscule comfort it offered me.

I had killed someone.

It was like my brain didn't know how to deal with that. I couldn't stop picturing the image of Lucius lying on the ground in a puddle of his own blood, his dead eyes staring up at me. And obviously, it was still having a similar effect on me physically. My skin felt flushed, and I was breaking out in goose bumps. My heart was racing, and I couldn't seem to catch my breath.

Maybe I should wake up Jeremy, I decided. Maybe a little comfort from him would go a long way.

I turned to look at him still lying there. And I stared at him for a moment. I looked at the shape of his hard pecs and rippling abs. I looked at his strong arms, and the biceps in them. I looked at the shape of his face, and his lips, which begged me to kiss them. I looked at his dick, hanging there, calling for me to take it in my hands, caress it, show my love to it…

What the hell? A second ago I was overwhelmed with guilt, and now all of a sudden I was horny? And I didn't mean just like typical, everyday horny, like I got whenever I would curl up with him in his bed. This was like I wanted to jump on him and ride him like a bull at a rodeo.

And still my heart was racing, and my skin felt hot and prickly.

Oh, fuck.

I forced myself to look away as it hit me what was going on. I got up and hurried over to a tree, which I planted myself against as I tried in vain to catch my breath.

I heard Jeremy starting to grunt as he woke up. "Evelyn?" he asked, seeing me leaning against the tree, panting. "Are you okay?"

"Please, don't make me look at you," I pleaded. "If I do, I don't know if I'll be able to control myself!"

"What do you mean?"

I took a few panting breaths before I answered, "I'm in heat."

I heard him getting up to his feet. "For real?"

"With everything going on, I completely lost track of my biological calendar!" I panted.

"So you don't want to…"

"Oh, I want to!" I nodded, barely stopping myself from turning my head to look at him. "I want to like you wouldn't believe!"

"But you don't want to want to because…"

"Because if we do, you'll most likely knock me up!"

There was a long pause, during which I continued fighting to stop myself from turning around and jumping him. I could just feel his presence, even from several feet away, and it was all I could do not to maul him.

And then he started to laugh.

I finally actually turned around and looked at him again, forgetting about my struggle as my lust was momentarily tempered. "What?" I demanded.

"This is perfect!" he said. "It's just what we need!"

"What are you talking about?"

"If anything can bring the two packs together, this can," he said. "A pup born of both packs!"

I blinked, staring at him. "You're serious!"

"Isn't that what you want?" he said, coming ever closer, causing my pulse to speed up. "You wanted us to have pups together, didn't you? And if it's both of ours, then it's a child that both packs can love! Is there anything better to bring them together?"

If I hadn't been panting with lust at that point, I might have started to cry happy little tears. "You still haven't given up hope?"

"Would I be the guy you fell in love with if I did?"

No. He really wouldn't have.

And once I realized that, I stopped trying to fight the urges stampeding through me.

I sprang up into his arms, throwing my arms and legs around him, and kissing him like I'd never kissed him before. He carried me back over to the spot where we'd just woken up, and lowered me back down to the ground, laying me out on my back. "You're sure you're ready for this?"

Oh, come on, I'd just let go of all my hesitation! I didn't want to pick it up again now! "Don't talk," I commanded. "Let's just fuck!"

We wasted little time on foreplay. I didn't have the patience for it. I was hot and bothered and ready to go. Oh, Jeremy tried. He started out kissing my neck and collar, feeling up my boobs and fingering my slit. But when he felt how wet I was already—not to mention the way I kept impatiently fidgeting beneath him—I think he figured out that I didn't need warming up.

So he knelt over me, taking me into his arms and slid inside me almost too easily. Almost immediately, I captured him in my legs, holding him deep inside me as he started to thrust. I pulled at him with my legs, urging his thrusts on, almost using him as a masturbatory tool, even from beneath him. My arms came up to embrace—no, *ensnare* him, pulling him down onto my chest.

I was so hot I was able to orgasm after only the first five minutes, and was well on my way to another within minutes after that. After the first twenty minutes, by which point I had rolled us over to put myself on top at least three times, I'd managed to get myself off at least five times. And I was a long way from done.

Even after he finally released his seed inside me, I wasn't even close to sated. Once he pulled out, I bent over and took him into my mouth, sucking him like a hungry Hoover. I actually found myself getting impatient at how long it took to get him back up to full hardness; hell, why couldn't he just keep going after firing off? Why did we have to stop?

But I eventually got him back up for more and what would end up being our all-day marathon continued.

We did it in every position conceivable. Each time he got off, we took a short break, during which he would ask if I was done yet. To which I would answer him by taking him into my mouth and sucking him back to hardness. I don't doubt after a while I was starting to seriously wear him out. But like a trooper, he kept up with my out-of-control libido for as long as it took to satisfy it.

By the time it started to get dark again, I decided I was finally spent. Jeremy let out a big breath when I told him that, which sounded like relief. I curled up against him, tenderly stroking his face. "Poor guy," I said. "I really put you through the ringer today, didn't I?"

"I didn't know you had that kind of energy in that little body," he said.

"Well, you've got some kind of stamina to keep up with me," I said. Then I kissed him tenderly. "Thank you for this."

He cradled me in his arms, staring at my face. "I love you, Evelyn," he said.

I think that was the first time I'd heard him say it out loud.

I lovingly kissed him a few more times before we curled up and went back to sleep, resting off our day's exertion, while I took one hand and cradled my belly, thinking about what we had just created. In every sense.

*

We got up well into the night hours, and made the decision to start making our way back the way we came. The idea of returning once again was not an easy choice to make. After all, which pack did we go to? The one I had just escaped from, that wanted to force us apart? Or the one that banished us, that I had just killed a member of?

We weren't going to come up with the answer all at once, so we hoped it would come to us on the way. We stopped to hunt for some food, catching a few raccoons to eat on the way, which gave us some more time to think. And still a decision continued to elude us.

But then around dawn, we heard a howl come from the direction of the Morgandorf village. And I could recognize the howl, too.

It was Leon.

If he was in the Morgandorf village, this had to mean trouble. We started hurrying in that direction, confident now that the decision had been made for us. And whatever was happening there, we were also confident that we had to get to it fast.

We finally came to a stop on top of a hill overlooking the village, where through the trees we could see the confrontation going down. And it was massive. It looked like nearly the entire Caldour pack had come out in force to face their enemy, and nearly the entire Morgandorf pack stood at attention facing them back.

And what's more, it sounded like they were talking about me.

"You can search all you want," Ricardo was saying. "She's not here. The sooner you realize that and move on, the easier it'll be for all of us."

"Don't try to confuse us!" That was my dad speaking. "We know how you all brainwashed her! You turned her into… into one of you! You got her to turn against her own pack, and now you're hiding her!"

"That girl was never one of us!" one of the Morgandorfs said. "She was a liar! A fake!"

"And now she's killed one of ours!" Ricardo added. "If anything, I'd say she's proven herself a true Caldour. She's as much an enemy of the Morgandorf pack now as any of you!"

"Don't fall for it, Leon!" one of the Caldours said.

"Even if she's not here, I say we tear this whole place apart, just to be sure!"

Several of the Morgandorfs growled in response, some of them shifting to their four-legged forms, preparing to meet an attack.

That's when Charlene stepped forward, taking Leon by the arm. "Leon, please, this has gone far enough!"

Leon only shoved her aside. "Not yet."

Both packs stood their grounds, staring the other down. Left and right they started shifting to their four-legged forms, preparing to charge. Leon and Ricardo stood meeting each other's gaze as both their features started taking lupine shape, adding to the ferocity of their scowls.

And so, before this could go any further, I made my presence known. I reared my head back and howled, calling for everyone to stop. And seconds later, Jeremy's voice joined me, our song bringing the two sides to a momentary stop.

We came running down the hill, moving in between the two packs, stopping right in the path between Leon and Ricardo. We each shifted back to our two-legged forms, as I faced my pack, and Jeremy faced his.

"Evelyn!" my dad gasped. "We thought you were…"

"Everyone, please!" I called. "This all has to stop!"

"Not while they're still here!" Leon declared.

"You don't speak for us!" Ricardo commanded. "You never did!"

I looked around at all the faces around me. Faces I knew and loved. Family I had grown up with on the Caldour side. Friends I had made on the Morgandorf side. "I have something to tell you all!" I called. "I went into heat yesterday. Jeremy and I are going to have a pup."

Several gasps went up all around us.

"A pup of both Morgandorf and Caldour blood," Jeremy said. "Something to unite us both."

"No!" my dad growled, pushing his way through the pack to advance on me. "No, no, no, NOOOO! You've betrayed me in enough ways, but this…! This is unconscionable! My grandchild is supposed to be the future leader of the Caldour pack! You are not going to—"

"Rene, shut up!"

Everyone whirled around to the sound of my mom's voice as she emerged. "There are bigger things at stake here than your childish pride! Our daughter has made her choice! Have the goddamn decency to respect that!"

Dad looked at her in shock, as if he didn't know how to deal with his wife standing up to him.

"Evie?" I heard Andrea's voice call. I turned to see her running past the crowd of her pack.

Ricardo turned and pointed. "Get her back to her room!" he commanded.

"No!" Jeremy shouted. "Let her stay! Let everyone stay! This concerns all of you!"

"You're pregnant?" Andrea probed.

I smiled at her, and nodded. "I don't want my pup to live with both sides of its family fighting and killing each other!" I said. "My pup should be able to live in peace, without worrying about pack allegiances, or being attacked! Isn't that what all of you want? What do all of you want for your pups? We've all been brought up on this feud, taught to hate each other, and we've kept fighting for all this time! How much longer are we going to keep passing on this legacy of hate?"

"You're an idealistic girl, Evelyn," Ricardo said. "But ideals can't undo the past. They won't bring back the lives that have been taken!"

"Neither will taking more lives!" Jeremy said. "But maybe they can prevent more death."

"This is funny, coming from you!" Brock snapped. "Lucius is dead because of you!"

"Lucius is dead because he attacked us!" I said. "The last thing I wanted was to kill him, but I acted to save someone else's life." Then I looked up and pointed to Charlene. "Hers."

The whole Caldour pack turned to stare at Charlene, who looked around at them uncomfortably. "Oh, come on, do you have to put me on the spot like this?"

"Everyone here," I called, "I know you all. Old Tobias, you used to bounce me on your knee and sing songs to me when I was little! Jana, remember the party when we were thirteen, when you dared me to go up and kiss Tucker?" Then I turned to the Morgandorfs. "Tara, you were one of the first friends I made in the Morgandorf pack. I was afraid no one in your pack would accept me, but you came right up and made me feel at home." Then I paused, as Andrea stepped up to the front of the Morgandorf crowd. "And Andrea…"

I turned to the Caldours suddenly, pointing at the teenage girl before me. "Is that the face of your enemy? This little girl? Even after the Morgandorfs found me out and banished me, she stayed on my side all the way! The daughter of the Morgandorf alpha, and she doesn't even have any conception of hate! Why should she have to be involved in a war?"

"She's right," Charlene said, finally stepping forward to join us.

"Charlene?" Leon said, startled.

"I was just like all of you," she said. "I always judged the Morgandorfs based on the stories I'd heard. All this crap that we've passed around for years to demonize each other. But look at them! All of you, look at the other side!"

"They're all just like you!" I said. "They have families! Homes! Pups! This forest is more than big enough for us all! What do we have to fight over?"

And all around me, it looked like I was actually having an effect. Everyone seemed to be stopping to think, and were busy talking amongst each other.

"We don't expect you all to start liking each other," Jeremy said. "We're not naïve enough to think it'll be that simple. But can't this pup be a start?"

Most of the hostile faces that had been present a minute ago had begun to vanish. Everyone was looking more thoughtful now.

Most of them, anyway.

"All right, that's enough!" Dad said, stepping up to me. "We're done with this drivel! You're going to come back home with me where—"

"Rene!" Leon commanded. Then he paused, and said, "Give it up. It's over."

"But she—"

"I said, give it up! She's beyond your authority now."

Dad actually looked... the only word I can think to describe it is "helpless."

"Come on, everyone," my mom said to the Caldour pack. "Let's go home."

They all started turning and walking away. Not a drop of blood had been spilled.

On the other side, the Morgandorfs started heading back to their homes. Only Andrea stayed behind, rushing forward to embrace me.

I turned my head to see Charlene having also hung behind. "I wouldn't have believed it, but that actually worked!"

"It's just a start," Jeremy said. "We're not going to end generations of hate in one day."

"But we got them to not fight," I said. "I'd call that a win. And I don't think we'll need to worry about them hunting us anymore."

"But where will you go now?" Charlene asked. "Even if you come back home, I don't think Jeremy will be very welcome there. Or you with the Morgandorfs. Where will you live?"

I smiled down at Andrea, stroking her hair. "Wherever we want."

*

EPILOGUE

The pups were starting to play a little rough. It had been amusing at first, watching them jump and tumble around with that squeaky little rubber alien with the big googly eyes, but now two of them had the squeak toy in their jaws and were playing a little tug-o-war with it, threatening to tear it in two, while the third was eagerly coming up to snatch it away from both of them.

It was at that point that I decided to step in and mediate the game. "Hey, now," I said, getting up from my lawn chair and stepping over to them. "If you can't play nice, I'm going to have to take your toys away. No more fighting," I said as I knelt down and took hold of the little green thing in their jaws, which they calmly released and let me take, looking up at me with meek eyes. "What did I tell you all?"

At that question, the three little furry, four-legged creatures before me rose up, shifting into their two-legged forms and standing before me with humbled looks. "Fighting is bad," said the seven-year-old girl with the little brown curls. "Fighting gets people hurt."

"That's right, Lana," I nodded. "And what do people who fight get?"

"No dessert," said all three of them in the same monotone expression.

"That's right!" I said, pointing a finger at them. "So what are you all going to do now?"

"Play nice," they drawled.

"Very good," I smiled. "Maybe we should get some more toys out for each of you, so you don't have to fight over them. Is that okay?"

The kids smiled and nodded. "I want my bouncy ball, mommy!" said little four-year-old Amy.

"I'm gonna get my super soaker!" said five-year-old Barry.

I was about to tell him not to shoot his sisters with it, but decided a little water play wouldn't hurt anyone. "Sure, have fun," I said.

I sat back down in the lawn chair next to Jeremy, as the kids went to fetch their toys. "You sure about that?" he said. "You remember what he did the last time you let him play with that."

"What's the matter?" I smirked. "Afraid of a little splash?"

I lifted my head and sniffed the air, as I detected Andrea's scent approaching, moments before I saw her step around the corner. "Hi guys," she said.

"Hey, everybody, look who's here!" I told the kids. The girls immediately ran cheering for her, while Barry hung back for a moment. Andrea ducked down and picked up the happy, squealing Amy, while Lana came up and hugged her leg.

"You on spring break already?" Jeremy asked. "And you come back here of all places?"

"You think there's any pace I'd rather be?" she smiled, bouncing the giggling Amy in her arms.

"Hey, Auntie Andie!" Barry said, suddenly stepping up with his super soaker in hand, and shooting her with a face-full of water. Andrea sputtered and shook her head.

I chuckled at her expense. "There just might be," I said.

Andrea glared playfully at Barry. "You're asking for it, buster!" she warned, letting Amy down. "Now I'm gonna have to CHASE YOU!"

The pups screamed with delight as Andrea went running after them. I watched with a big smile, as Jeremy reached out for my hand. "You still wishing your dad could see this?"

I sighed, letting my smile fade. "I haven't spoken to him since the day he said I wasn't his daughter anymore. And I'm not counting on that changing any time soon."

"Don't tell me you've given up?" he said. "We never would've made peace between the packs if you ever did that before."

I thought about it briefly, before saying, "Maybe I haven't totally forgiven him yet, either."

"Maybe it's time to try," he suggested. "The least you can do is give him a call."

Jeremy always did have a big heart. That's what I loved about him.

It took me a while to get the nerve, but I did eventually get up from the chair. I walked inside the house, found my phone, and taking a breath, dialed my dad's number.

THE END

Message From The Author:

Thanks so much for reading all the way to the end, I really hope you enjoyed it. If you did I would love it if you could leave me a rating. This helps other people find my books :)

*Details of the **mailing list** and other books by the Simply Shifters camp are on the following pages :)*

Jasmine x x

*

Get Yourself a FREE Bestselling Paranormal Romance Book!

Join the "**Simply Shifters**" Mailing list today and gain access to an exclusive **FREE** classic Paranormal Shifter Romance book by one of our bestselling authors along with many others more to come. You will also be kept up to date on the best book deals in the future on the hottest new Paranormal Romances. We are the HOME of Paranormal Romance after all!

* Get FREE Shifter Romance Books For Your Kindle & Other Cool giveaways

* Discover Exclusive Deals & Discounts Before Anyone Else!

* Be The FIRST To Know about Hot New Releases From Your Favorite Authors

Click The Link Below To Access Get All This Now!

SimplyShifters.com

Already a subscriber? OK, just turn the page :)

ALSO BY SIMPLY SHIFTERS PUBLISHING....

SOLD TO THE DRAGONS

#1 Paranormal Romance Bestseller

In a dystopian future, fertile women are so hard to come by that they are now bought and sold for huge sums of money across the world. You could say that women are the new currency.

Curvy Kira Southerly is one of the few remaining fertile women left on the planet and she has resigned herself to the fate of being SOLD.

However, she had no idea she would end up being sold to two young and handsome bachelors named Blake and Steven. They are both dragon shifters and they are intent on mating with her and producing a baby as soon as possible.

With not enough fertile women to go around the brothers have no choice but to share the curvy beauty among themselves. Something that allows Kira to fulfill her every sexual fantasy....

Being sold to dragons should not be this much fun, should it?